NOTHING
A novel by Dorothea Kreklow .

ISBN 978-0-6151-7891-2

This novel is dedicated to m y children
Shannon B eedle and Shaw n K reklow .

'There is, in most of us, a dark space, a place we never wish to visit...but sometimes we have no choice.'
Excerpt from an essay by D.Clive Dunn.

Mark Down, stood in front of his latest work of art, a beautiful landscape of the rolling, golden wheat fields of Eastern Washington with a brilliant, cloudless blue sky for a background. He was pleased with the painting and signed the lower left hand corner in a neatly printed line. The line of his brush strokes clean and simple, the letters of his name looked like a little row of stiff soldiers. The paint would be dry by morning and he would take this picture and several others to a gallery where his oils sold really well.

Maureen was bored. She was waiting for her furniture to be delivered. She had sold her old house in the country and bought a townhouse on the outskirts of Seattle. She was single, in her mid-forties, pale skinned with watery blue eyes with light brown eyes. She was happily looking forward to starting her new job in an upscale art dealer's gallery. She hummed to herself and then sang out loud, "I've got plenty on nothing, and nothing's plenty for me." *That's just silly,* she thought, I have a cup, tea bags and a kettle, *that's not nothing. It's almost nothing but at least I can make a cup of tea!* She stood in the living room looking out of the window and there still was no sign of a moving van parked in front of her new home. Just a minute, she thought, If the cup and *tea bags and kettle were 'not nothing' did that mean the two negatives canceled out each* other out and the things she had, actually were something? She realized that she had better stop playing these word games otherwise she would go crazy. Sometimes when it came to interacting with people these crazy thoughts would pop into her head and sometimes spew out of her mouth. It was pretty funny really, to watch their reactions and see them take a step away from her and then make mumbled reasons for exiting her presence. I hate waiting, I hate empty spaces, I hate not being able to go out, I hate *having to do one thing when I want to do something else. If I went out I'd bet a hundred dollars that the moving van would arrive when I'm gone. Is this room spinning?*

Then the waiting was over and the Ace Moving Van was parking in front of her townhouse and three able bodied young men jumped out and opened the rear door and pulled down a ramp. One of them walked to the front door, carrying a clipboard, he raised his hand to ring the bell. He jumped slightly when the response to his ring was instantaneous as the door was pulled open even before he lowered his arm. He faced Maureen who was fluffing her hair as she stepped back to allow him access to the house.

"Mornin' Ma'am, This shouldn't take no time at all." Oh geez, does this mean it will take some time, or will it be instantly unloaded?

"I'm in no hurry at all young man. Oh I see your name is Jerry." She smiled at Jerry as she touched his name-tag on the front of his shirt. "I'll show you precisely where to put all my pieces." Jerry took a step back and turned to the two other movers and nodded for them to start to unload Maureen's furniture. Maureen acted as if the moving men were simple and constantly cautioned them to be careful not to drop anything or scratch her precious antique pieces. She made the men feel very uncomfortable. It was as if a weirdness emanated from her. Within reason they worked as fast and as carefully as they could, but her hovering only hampered them instead of helping. Finally every piece of furniture was positioned in the five rooms to her satisfaction and she signed the release forms and the three men went hastily toward the moving van. To tip or not to tip, that is the question. She raised her hand toward the men and called, "Yoo hoo, I have something for you." Tip. She handed the clipboard man a five dollar bill, "Go buy your-selves a latte each." She smiled like an angel who was showering the little people of the world with precious gifts. The lead moving man said, "Thanks." Cheap bitch!

Maureen spent the rest of her day unwrapping ornaments and placing them where she thought they looked their best. Then she carefully picked out the clothes she would wear to the new job she would be starting the next day. She chose a smart rose-colored suit that made her pale skin reflect a pinkish glow. She coordinated grey high-heeled shoes with a chic grey silk neck scarf. After that she took a long hot bubble bath and found herself singing over and over again, "One two buckle my shoe, one two buckle my shoe…." Continuing her chant she stepped out of the tub, toweled off and went to bed. She had previously set her alarm clock for six a.m.

She arrived at the Gallery Gallactica at eight 'o clock after stopping at a fast food place for coffee and a doughnut. She was welcomed by the owner and introduced to three other staff members. They all seemed very nice and she was shown to her small desk in a back room and encouraged to study the inventory of artworks and their values. Then she had a lesson in hanging pictures and changing the angles of spotlights to show the pictures at their very best. Time flew by and she was anxious to make her first sale. She would be earning a small salary, but the big money came from the commission she would earn from a sale. There was a catch, isn't there always one? She was the junior member and would only get a customer if the three other associates were already involved in a sale.

After working in the gallery for about a month Maureen became comfortable with the routines and her fellow employees. However she was shy and avoided socializing with them as when she did she tended to babble and embarrass herself. She was good with customers and made some very profitable sales for the gallery.

One day her boss called her into his office and sat Maureen down for a talk.

"Maureen you seem to be doing your job rather well. Any problems?" Does that mean that there is a problem? Maureen wondered to herself.

"No sir, no problems. I do enjoy working here. Is there something wrong?" Bill had a friendly well-tanned face and was dressed in a suit with a perky little spotted bow tie. His grey hair was perfectly combed and parted on one side.

"Call me Bill. It's just that I notice that you don't socialize with the rest of the staff. We like to think of ourselves as more of a family than a work unit. Are you sure you are comfortable with the job?" She said she was and then he brought up another subject. "Well I'm pleased to hear that Maureen. I do have a big favor to ask you. One of the artists we sell for is a bit difficult when we reject any of his artworks. Most of his stuff sells really well, but on occasion he brings in a painting, that to be frank, is a bit over the edge. He's bringing in some new canvases this afternoon and I'd like you to select and hang what he brings in. Don't be shy about refusing any of his work, but be prepared for him to get a bit rude or even angry if he feels rejected. His name is Mark Down. Do you think you can handle that?"

This is a test. At the tone you will be instructed to go to the emergency channel on your fm radio station.

"I don't see that being a problem Bill. And thank you for having so much faith in me." Maureen stood and smiled and left Bill's office. He thought I hope she handles him better than the others did.

A two p.m. the gallery was deserted except for Maureen who was holding down the fort while the others were enjoying a long lunch. The bell on the door tinkled as a light haired, lean and handsome man came through it. He was pushing a dolly holding a dozen or so fabric covered paintings. They were large in size, suitable for hanging on a wall behind a couch. Maureen walked toward him with a smile and an outstretched hand. "Hi I'm Maureen and you must be Mark Down, the famous painter. I was expecting you."

"Right then let's get to it. Just call me Mark I don't stand on ceremony." He quickly uncovered the paintings and lined them up along an empty wall. "If I do say so myself, they are all Masterpieces and they should all bring in my usual fee. Okay then I'll be going. I just need for you to sign for them." A bit stunned by his brusque and speedy delivery, Maureen told him she would have to look at them for a few minutes to see if the gallery would accept all of them. She stepped back and looked at the row of stunning, beautiful landscapes. Then because the pictures were lined up against a white wall she saw that the end picture was a plain white canvas. It looked as if it was prepped with gesso and accidentally included in the line-up.

"Sir, Mark, you'll probably want to take this one back with you, unless of course you are going to call it 'snow.'" She was laughing and she never made jokes, and it was possible that this was her first, but instead of laughing along with her Mark Down's face turned beet red, along with his scalp which glowed pink through his pale hair, and he exploded,

"Are you trying to insult me? This one's called 'Nothing' it's beyond me why you can't see that, when it is right in front of your face. I'll be talking to Bill about this." *I'll lose my job.*

"I am so sorry, I do see that the painting is nothing, and of course we'll take it. My mistake. I'll sign for all of them and give you a receipt." She hastily signed and ushered Mark out of the store.

I'm an idiot. I should have stood my ground. Now what the hell am I going to do? Hoping that the rest of the employees wouldn't be back too soon Maureen grabbed a sheet of bubble wrap and took the blank canvas out the back door to the employee parking lot and shoved it into the trunk of her car. When the rest of the staff returned she had hung the new paintings and arranged spot-lights so they were shown off to their best advantage. Bill, her boss, congratulated her and enquired if Mark had been difficult at all. She replied that everything had gone just fine. *How on earth will I explain the missing picture,* she thought and decided she would think about it later.

That evening when she got home she kicked of her shoes, she was worn out. After she got in the house and put the kettle on for tea she remembered the canvas. With a sigh she fetched it from her car and leaned it against the wall in her living room. She made the tea and took it to an easy chair where she sat, sipped it and stared at the bubble wrapped trouble. She got up and removed the wrap and started to squeeze each bubble until they broke with a loud snap. *Snap, snap, snap, I'm in a trap, snap, snap, snap.*

8

When all the bubbles had burst Maureen had chanted the little rhyme many times over. With a feeling of disgust for having brought the stupid thing home she got up and walked over to the blank canvas and gave it a light kick. Her shoe seemed to enter into nothingness and the foot disappeared at her ankle. She gulped and quickly pulled her foot away. *What the hell was that? I am so tired I'm imagining things. I'd better eat something.*

Maureen tossed a Lean Cuisine frozen dinner in the micrwave and removed it when the timer dinged. She gobbled it down and went back to where the picture of nothing leaned against the wall. She knelt down in front of it and touched it with her finger. She pushed her finger forward and it vanished like her foot had done. *It feels like nothing! It's empty space. This is impossible.* She pulled her finger back and looked it over. It seemed to be okay. She plunged her arm in and pulled it back out. *I wonder what it looks like in there. Maybe I'll just put my head in and take a look.* She pushed her head through the canvas and couldn't see anything. She leaned forward and fell into the nothingness.

****

A week later after the artist had contacted him and asked for the picture frame back, Bill filled out a missing persons report and told the police officer that she had probably stolen the missing painting, sold it and taken off. The investigating officer, Roger Brown, was dispatched to Maureen's townhouse and had to make a forced entry. His brow furrowed and his intelligent face looked mystified as he raked his hand through his slightly thinning straight black hair. He looked around and found her purse in the kitchen, it held her ID. and some money and she was now here to be found. He wrote up a report and basically it said he found no one and no evidence of foul play. He also said there was a picture frame leaning against a wall, it probably belonged to the gallery but there was no picture in it. He contacted

Bill and told the gallery owner that he could go the townhouse and retrieve it. Bill declined, and said the artist had been trying to palm off that picture of 'Nothing' on him for several years. The case was left open pending further developments because there was really nothing to report.

2.

There had been no signs that M aureen w ould ever turn up again. She had
been gone alm ost six m onths.

So the bank that had given her the loan to buy the townhouse declared it
abandoned and put it up for sale along w ith its contents. B etty, a plum p m iddle-aged
bleached, straw berry blond, real estate agent w ho w as handling the sale for the
bank, considered buying the place herself as she found the furnishings quite
appealing. She changed her m ind w hen she w alked past the em pty picture fram e.
The hairs had prickled up on the back of her neck and a slight nausea had overcom e
her. L ittle beads of sw eat had rim m ed the outline of her lips and her plum p cheeks
had turned rosy. Som etim es she w ondered w hy she had started a new career in real
estate at her advanced years. Well fifty wasn't that old anymore and it wasn't
physically dem anding and the m oney w as good. She didn't connect these feelings
w ith the blank picture fram e. She thought the bad vibes cam e from the townhouse
itself. This m orning she w as going to show the property to a young couple, new ly
m arried and excited to be buying their first hom e.

B rian and M andy arrived prom ptly at ten a.m . B oth w ere blue-eyed blonds,
skinny, w earing jeans and sw eats. They looked like tw ins. They fell in love w ith the
tow nhouse and its contents im m ediately. M andy squealed childishly about how

11

adorable this and that was and then occasionally commented that some of the things might have to go. Brian acted suitably impressed and agreed the furniture was great but some elements of the place were a bit girlish for his taste and a few things would have to go. They didn't argue over what would stay or go and Betty made the easiest and smoothest sale of her career. The couple had been pre-approved for a loan so there was no reason why they could not move in even before the paperwork was complete.

A few days later Brian and his new wife moved into their new home. Mandy wanted to re-arrange the furniture while Brian set up their computers in the spare bedroom. Suddenly there
were peals of laughter emanating from the living room. Brian stopped what he was doing and went to see what was so amusing to Mandy.

"Honey, look." She inclined her head toward the blank frame. It had been leaning against the wall behind the couch which Mandy had been shoving around to different places in the room. She was trying to see where it looked best to her. "Why would anyone want a blank picture frame?"

"It's not blank it's a picture of snow! Anyone can tell that." They looked at each other and burst out laughing. "You want me to hang it somewhere?"

"No that's okay. Maybe we could use the frame for when we find a picture we both like. Why don't you take it with you to the spare room." They both went back to what they had been doing, Brian whistling happily and Mandy considering pushing the couch back to its original position. When they were done they went grocery shopping and both exclaimed at how expensive groceries were.

"We won't always spend this much because we won't need to always buy stuff like flour and sugar. I think it was all those exotic spices that you insisted that we needed Brian."

"You'll thank me when I make my famous Brian's Booming Baked Bean Casserole, guaranteed to make you fart."

Mandy doubled over laughing, "Shut up! Someone will hear you. Is there a bathroom in this store? I could have waited till we got home if you hadn't made me laugh."

After they left the grocery store they looked at some poster-size pictures at a local frame shop and discussed which would look best in their frame.

"You think we should measure it first?" queried Mandy.

"No, your genius husband can eye anything and know it's the right size without the need to measure. Besides if the frame is too small we can cut the picture to fit it."

"What if the picture is too small for the frame?"

"You worry too much. Trust me."

They picked a black and white picture of a male skier. He looked for all the world as if he was going to come flying out of the picture into the face of whoever was viewing it. They drove home happily chatting about the new poster picture and where they would hang it after Brian put it in the frame. They decided the wall across from the front door. That way they would see it every time they came home and encourage them to save for a skiing trip.

A week after the newlyweds moved into the townhouse they had to go back to work. Mandy was a hairstylist and Brian was the manager of a local hardware store. They fell into a routine and after a very few weeks they hardly glanced at the picture of the skier in the picture frame that had come with the house. Until one Saturday morning when Mandy was dusting and Brian was playing computer games she called out,

"Brian, come look at this."

"Just a sec let me finish my game."

"No. Now Brian. Don't make me sound like your Mom here!"
She was standing in front of the skier picture frowning. Brian crept up behind her and pinched her bottom.

"You don't feel like my Mom."

"Brian! You pinch your Mom's butt?" Brian put his arms around her and nuzzled her neck.

"No I don't do that. Now what was so important that you made me lose my game?"

"It's probably nothing. But look at this picture. It's kind of bulging out at the bottom away from the frame. Like maybe someone was trying to push a hole in it from behind."

"It looks okay to me, but I'll take it down and straighten it out. I could have used a bit more tape when I first did it. Then can I get back to my game?" That evening they went out to dinner and then spent the following day at the mall and took in a movie and before they knew it a new work-week had started.

A few hours after they left for work the skier picture began to bulge from the back into the hallway. It looked like a fist was trying to punch a hole in it. Then a scrawny almost fleshless hand did brake through, it was followed by a head and the emaciated body of Maureen, she tumbled out of the picture and fell to the floor. The picture was left looking as if the skier had burst out and landed in the room. She looked down at herself and her once smart suit was in tatters and hung like it was ten sizes too big. Her shoes were missing and her usually neat, coifed hair was hanging in gnarled dirty strands. She was shivering and hungry and in a state of disorientation. This looked like her new town house, her things were there but in different places. And also things were added that she knew didn't belong to her. She couldn't worry about that now she needed to get something to eat and really needed a hot cup of tea.

The kitchen was different with pantry, cupboards and fridge filled with foods she would never buy. It didn't matter at that moment she just needed to eat and figure out what was happening. She ate some soup and a sandwich and then her stomach hurt as if it had never experienced food before. This was disconcerting so she put her head in her hands and waited for the sensations to go away. Eventually she felt a little better and decided to look around her home which was now so different. It was obvious that two people now lived there, a guy and a woman, she surmised after looking in the closets. There were things she knew she had never owned, a big T. V, Cd's and stereo. There were two computers in the spare room. She went back into the living room and lay on the couch in a state of pure exhaustion. She was asleep in seconds.

Brian usually arrived home about a half hour before Mandy at around five p. m. He would kick off his shoes and go straight to the computer, turn it on, read his e-mail and then play games until it was time to help Mandy with dinner. This day was no different than any other so that's what he did. When Mandy arrived home she kicked off her shoes and started to yell, "I'm home" as she usually did but today as she was removing her shoes she looked up and the broken picture jumped out at her. Where the hell is the skier? She thought, Has he skied out of the picture?

"Brian are you home?" There was hysteria in her voice and when Brian heard her his reply was immediate.

"Yes Hon, are you all right?" She thought to give her usual answer to that question, "No silly, I'm half left!" But she didn't, her voice trembled and she said, "Can you come here a minute?" He had anticipated the request and was instantly beside her. "

"Holy Shit! What happened to our skier? Someone tore a hole in the picture!"

"This is creepy, we should call the police." Mandy added.

"Hang on," he took her hand, "we should check things out first. Stay behind me."

Slowly, holding hands and staying very close to each other they first crept into the kitchen.

"Look at that," said Mandy, "someone ate in here, there are crumbs on the counter, an empty soup bowl and the cupboard doors are open. They turned and went to the living room and there lying on the couch and quietly snoring was the wraithish figure of a middle-aged woman. "What shall we do? I wouldn't have minded her breaking in to eat something, but she didn't have to screw with our picture." Mandy was whispering. "Wake her up Brian."

"You wake her. I'd probably frighten her!"

"You wake her. I'll call the police." By this time their voices were rising and Maureen began to stir and then she sat up with a jerk.

"Who the hell are you two? What are you doing living in my house?"

"This is our house," chimed Brian and Mandy together.

Maureen jumped up and then tottered weakly, the young couple both stepped forward to steady her. They decided to all go into the kitchen and have a talk to understand what was going on. Mandy vowed to herself that if the freaky woman made one strange move she would dial 911 and get the police to haul her away.

Mandy graciously made them all hot tea, and then asked the women to explain herself. A lot put out, Maureen huffily let them know that it was they who should be doing the explaining. Brian quietly suggested that Maureen give them her name and tell them the last thing she remembered. She did and Brian then asked if she could tell them what date that had happened. Maureen almost passed out when she was told that was almost seven months ago. Brian was very skeptical and told Maureen that he had used the frame for the skier picture and he hadn't fallen in. How could she explain that.

"I can't. I shouldn't have to! Maybe it's because you were framing it from the back, and you weren't standing in front of it. But anyway I'll show you that the picture frame is like an open door." The three of them marched out of the room and stood in front of the ruined picture of the skier. Maureen warily reached up and tore the ruined picture down to the frame edge. Then she knowingly looked at the young couple and plunged her arm into the gaping hole. It disappeared up to her shoulder. They gasped as one. Brian said,

"No way! That's impossible. Here let me try." He shouldered Maureen aside and pushed his own arm up to the shoulder. He pulled it out saying, "If I had felt the wall behind the picture, of course that would have made sense. This doesn't."

"Let me try," said Mandy, but before she did so Brian leaned all the way into the frame bending at the waist. She inched in beside him and leaned into the hole as well.

"You two be careful or you'll fall in like I did." Maureen weakly warned them. They both stood up and Brian said,

"What a rush, like standing on your head. What's in there Maureen?"

"I don't know. I don't remember anything about being in there. But I think I was scared a lot." Keep away from it. We should get hold of the authorities and have them destroy the frame."

"You're probably right, but I want to take one more look, it's not completely dark in there, it seemed to look sort of like twilight." Mandy was peeking in again and bent too far and started to fall in. Brian quickly grabbed her knees and tried to haul her out, but he seemed to be being dragged along with her. He screamed to Maureen to get over there and help him. To her credit she did courageously race to his side and grab the belt to his jeans, but he was heavy and before she could disentangle her grip on him she tumbled over the edge of the frame for a second time. Only muffled screams could be heard for a few seconds, but there was no one there to hear them.

3

Seated at his desk, Roger, the detective, once again found himself looking into a missing persons' report. The freaky thing was that the missing couple was from the same townhouse as that other missing person, Maureen someone who had left no traces as to what had happened to her. It was probably a coincidence. He paged his new assistant, Angela to come to his office. Once she was there he asked her to put together an investigation kit. To her utter delight he said she was to accompany him on what would be her first field trip experience with Roger. She was just out of college and had thought it would be forever before she actually went out on a case. She was eagerly collecting what was needed, smiling and pushing her pretty, brown curly hair behind one ear, and gave her boss adoring glances. Her hero worship of him was embarrassing for Roger, who was almost in his late forties and old enough to be her father his dark hair was starting to be peppered with grey, but he figured she would soon get over her adoration once she got used to the newness of the job. She would find that it was not the glamorous job depicted on various detective shows on television. She had yet to even see a dead body.

"What should I collect first?" Angela asked. Her nostrils flared as she smelled the musty air in the house. "Finger prints off all the door knobs? Hair from the combs in the bathroom?" She was so eager Roger put his finger to his lips to quiet her. That didn't stop her and she continued on, "Maybe I should get samples of food from the refrigerator. "

"Hold on. Don't touch anything until I ask you to. First we need to make notes on what we see before touching anything. You'll get a chance to take samples, but when I say so." Roger walked through the townhouse with Angela on his heels. When they got to the kitchen Roger said,

"Tell me what you see."

"A tidy kitchen with a soup cup and a plate in the sink and three cups on the table."

"Good. The couple obviously had a visitor and they sat together in the kitchen and drank tea or coffee together. That would indicate that they probably knew each other. The missing persons report only listed two people missing. They seemed to have gone missing a couple of weeks ago according to their parents and neighbors. Does anything strike you as strange, considering that there was a third person in the house with them?"

"No, everything looks pretty much in place to me."

"Don't you find that to be a bit curious? Well look around you again. Doesn't it strike you as odd that nothing is out-of-place. Their car keys are hanging on the kitchen hook. The woman's purse is on the hall table with money, ID. and credit cards all there."

"So they weren't robbed and there wasn't a fight or a struggle. They left willingly with the third person who was here." Angela seemed inordinately pleased with her deductions.

"It would seem so." Roger replied. "Let's look around one more time, then you can collect some samples for forensics."

"What do you make of this?" Angela called from the entry way of the townhouse.

"Well I'm not sure," said Roger as he eyed the torn picture of the skier. I don't think it can mean much. It looks like it was a cheap print. Perhaps they didn't like it and tore it to see if there was another picture behind it. Tell you what you can do, photograph the cups on the kitchen table before you lift the fingerprints. Then bag and label them along with the cups. I'm not sure if they will give us anything but we should check them out anyway. Did you know a woman also disappeared from this same townhouse about six or seven months back? Absolutely no hint of what happened to her. It's an open ended file and it looks a lot like this might be another one."

"How cool is that?" Bubbled Angela. "I love a good mystery."

"So do I, and our job is to solve them. I hope this doesn't turn out to be as unsolvable as the first one."

When they got back to the office Angela took the fingerprints and ran them through the F.B.I.'s data base to identify them. When she got the results she went and showed them to Roger. He looked them over and said,

"Nothing helpful here. They belong to the young couple Brian and Mandy, that's to be expected. The third set isn't on file anywhere. That's not unusual either. It looks like we're drawing a blank on this one too." Roger sighed. He asked Angela to file the notes and results as an open case.

****

Two months later Betty the real-estate sales woman was walking through the townhouse with Brian and Mandy's parents. They just wanted to keep some photos of their kids and a few childhood mementos that the couple had brought from their original families to become a part of their new life together. There were a lot of tears as the two sets of parents gathered these things together. They all agreed that the townhouse should be sold along with its furnishings. Their clothes should go to the

Goodwill and Betty agreed to take care of that chore. After the sad parents left Betty thought the bank should have the place cleaned and aired out and it would look pretty much the same as when she had first sold it to Brian and Mandy. On her way out she stopped by the picture frame with its tattered poster of a skier. She ripped it out all the way so it didn't look quite so tacky. Then she took the frame off the wall and stuffed it into the closet near the front door. As she attached the real estate lock on the front door she hoped that it would be the last time she had anything to do with this townhouse. She couldn't have put it into words what she felt about the place but one word, creepy, definitely came to mind.

4.

The townhouse stayed on the market for three more months. It was the beginning of fall and rain had set in making the place look gloomy. No one seemed to want it, possibly because the missing persons' stories had made the newspapers. Then a gossip tabloid had picked it up and stretched the truth beyond all reasoning. So as Betty once more showed the house and contents to a prospective buyer she silently prayed that the place would sell. She dreaded showing it. When she requested that another agent sell the house, her request was received with incredulity by her boss. He hinted that if she was so rich that she could forgo the hefty commission on a sale maybe she should retire or find herself another job elsewhere. She wanted to keep her job and so kept on showing the place.

"Well Mr. Prentice what do you think? Betty said brightly.

At six foot tall, tanned and in glowing good health, handsome with deep set, warm brown eyes with smile lines around them Harry said,

"You know I think this might do just fine." Betty let out an audible sigh of relief.

"The stories about this place don't bother you Mr. Prentice?" She felt compelled to ask.

"Call me Harry. No not really. For the last four years I've been in the most dangerous place in the world. Driving supply trucks between U S bases in Iraq. Before that I was in the army for twenty years. When I first joined I was in a bomb demolition squad, then I figured after ten years of that, I was lucky to still be alive so I transferred to military transport division. I think if I came out of that hell-hole in one piece, this disappearance story isn't going to scare me off." He smiled, his suntanned face crinkling with good humor. "I saved and invested enough, in my years over there, to not have to work for the rest of my life if I don't want to." Betty gave him a flirtatious wink followed by a breathless,

"Wow! That sure would be nice to be able to do that. What will you do with your time now?" Betty didn't really care what he did with his time, she was just being polite. She'd say and do almost anything to get rid of the townhouse.

"I think I'll write a book about all the corruption by the big U.S. supply companies, and I sure witnessed a lot of really sick stuff that some of our G.I.'s are getting away with. I figure if I write about it, it might go a long way toward putting a stop to the atrocities they commit under the guise of national security and helping those poor sons of bitches."

"I understand completely," simpered Betty as she stifled a yawn. But she didn't understand, and not only that, she wasn't interested in what happened in other parts of the world. Her immediate wish was to get the house sold and soon. She and Prentice went to her office and signed the sale papers and the deal was done.

Harry whistled as he padded around his new home. He felt he had completely lucked out with its already being furnished. He didn't care much for shopping for household items. Any old couch was good enough for him, just as long as he had one to sit on, a bed to sleep in, a stove to cook on and best of all two computers. What more could he want?   Hell, with such a good deal he might even consider finding someone nice to be Mrs. Prentice. It might be good to have a woman's touch around the house. He thought he'd really like to get started on his book before he went looking for a wife. It wouldn't hurt to sign up with one of those dating sites on the web though. But first he decided to take an inventory of the contents of the house. He thought that might be a good idea before he took out house insurance.

As he walked around the place listing the contents he chuckled to him self thinking this home owning thing sure was a far cry from what the rest of his life had been like. He left home at sixteen because his parents were abusive and drunk and fighting most of the time. He had a lot of friends and when he went to their houses he saw loving families and when compared to his he decided early on that he would never be like his parents. He slept in one of his friends' basement for the last couple of years of high school and paid rent with money he earned as a box boy in a local supermarket. After graduating he joined the army and saw a lot of the world having been stationed in Korea, the Middle East and a really fun two-year stint in Germany. After twenty years of that he left the army and became an independent trucker in Iraq. In four years he had made as much as he had been paid for twenty years in the army.

Harry soon settled into a routine. He got up early and went jogging for an hour. Got back home for breakfast and then spent the rest of the morning writing what he hoped would be an earth shattering exposé of what was really going on in Iraq, and what the American people were paying for with their tax dollars. He spent the rest of the day surfing the internet looking for facts to back up some of his assertions about how the U S wasted more money than was imaginable, abroad. The government had even sent over plane loads of cash and given it over to who knew who. It was just gone and no one could say where. Some evenings he would go to a local tavern and enjoy a beer with the locals. He enjoyed, for the first time in his life, being in a stable safe environment.

One day as Harry madly typed away on his manuscript he had a sense of something not quite right. He stopped typing and leaned back in his chair and thought he smelled something odd. It seemed to be carried by a breeze blowing through the room . *That's strange I'm sure there aren't any windows open,* he thought. Better go check it out. He stretched, raised his hands above his head and cracked his knuckles and stood. His knees cracked. Must be getting old, he thought. He took a huge sniff of the air and followed the odor to the front door closet. *Well I'll be damned I never noticed this closet before. I hope there isn't a dead dog in there.* He steeled himself and opened the door. Sure enough, that was where the smell was coming from, but he didn't know why it would be carried by a breeze. Where was the breeze coming from?

There were a lot of cold weather coats in the closet and Harry suspected they had been put in there while still damp from rain and no one had opened the door to the closet since. He went and got a big plastic garbage sack and began stuffing the coats along with their hangers into it. There were six coats and several scarves and gloves in the closet and he managed to get them all in the one bag. When all the coats were removed Harry saw the picture frame leaning against the back wall. *Well what have we here?* He thought as he reached in to pull it out. *That's odd, it's empty. I think this is a nice looking frame. Maybe I should look around for a picture to go in it.* He lifted it up in front of him and sniffed it to see if the smell had seeped into the wood of the frame. It didn't seem to smell bad so he leaned it against the wall opposite the front door and hauled the plastic garbage sack out to the garbage bins. *Mmm, I wonder which recycle bin I should put this stuff in. It's not glass or paper or food scraps or metal.* He dumped it in with the paper and hoped he wouldn't have an extra charge on his garbage bill.

Well I guess its back to the old computer and get writing, he thought. *Where did that draft come from?* He shrugged his shoulders and went back to work. But he couldn't concentrate after he sat down to write again. The odd smell was no longer wafting through the house but he got up and checked the closet once again. Nothing. Harry picked the picture frame up and once again sniffed it, but could not smell anything unusual. He thought he might hang the frame up in the room where he wrote, it needed something on the wall. It might inspire him as to what sort of picture he might buy. So he hooked his arm through the empty frame and practically freaked out when he saw that his arm wasn't visible on the other side of the frame. He quickly pulled his arm out and placed the frame on the floor. The floor should have shown through the frame but instead it just looked like the frame had an unpainted white surface. Holy shit! He exclaimed. He carefully put his foot on the surface of the frame and his foot looked as if it ended at his ankle. He quickly pulled it back out.

****

Mark Down was pacing back and forth in front of Bill, the gallery owner, demanding to be paid for his picture titled 'Nothing,' or if not, return the picture to Mark. Bill wasn't sure what to do. He, of course, didn't have the 'picture' if that's what the fool artist chose to call it. He did value having Mark's work, however difficult he might be, as the gallery took in a good deal of money from commissions on Mark's work. For all he knew the new owner of Maureen's house had probably sent it off to the dump.

"I'll tell you what Mark, I'll make some inquiries, no promises, and see if I can't find out what happened to it. If we can't trace it, then we will try and make sure you get some kind of compensation for it. Does that sound fair?"

Mark stopped pacing and rubbed his chin, his blond whiskers rasped like fine sand-paper, as if thinking about this offer. "No," he said, "I will expect to be paid the full price for that painting, less your commission of course. Does that not sound fair?"

"Give me a couple of days to think about it. Meanwhile did you have any new pictures for us?"

"There are three in my van, but how do I know that they won't conveniently go missing?"

"I won't take that remark in the spirit it was made. We have always been fair and honest with you. If you are not happy with this business relationship that we have, then I suggest you do business with another gallery." Bill hoped this wouldn't happen but he'd be damned if he would put up with how rude Mark always came across as being. Mark had in the past used a couple of other galleries and his artwork wasn't nearly as nicely displayed as it was in this gallery. He backed down a bit.

"Perhaps I'm being a bit difficult. I'll bring in my pictures and stop by in a couple of days to see if you've found out anything about my missing work." That was about as close to being reasonable as Mark had ever been. Mark thought, *I've got to get that picture back, and soon, before anything bad happens to someone.*

5.

Harry also paced back and forth, but in front of the picture frame lying on the floor. He tentatively put his foot into it again and it seemed to vanish just as it had before. He picked it up and rested it against the wall. As he was doing so his phone rang and he almost jumped out of his skin, the sound had so jarred his nerves. *My god I never thought I'd be so* jumpy about anything.

"Hullo," he said and noticed that his hands were visibly shaking. It was an old buddy from Iraq who had also driven in the same convoys as Harry.

"Harry, you old sand-dog, I thought I'd take you up on that offer to see your new digs and then we could get a beer and catch up and maybe talk about old times."

"Jimmy, my god it's great to hear from you. Sure, now I'm retired I have all the time in the world. When's it good for you?"

"Well sometime after two this afternoon. I took you at your word that it's great to be a home owner and I'll be checking out a couple of places not too far from where you live. I have some really terrific news I can't wait to tell you about as well."

Hearing from his old friend cheered Harry up and he shook off the creeped-out feeling he had been experiencing. He'd tell Jimmy about the frame and see what he had to say about it. Maybe the weird thing was all in his mind. But not so, his finger-tips were proof of that when they disappeared into nothingness when Harry checked just once more to see if it was his imagination working overtime. He put it back in the closet and leaned it against a side wall, then padded out to the kitchen to brew some coffee.

At a little after two Jimmy rang the bell and Harry let him in. After the usual 'heck how are you doing' greetings they settled themselves at the kitchen table and exchanged news about themselves. Harry didn't mention the frame and after a second cup of coffee Jimmy was fairly bursting with some news he wanted to tell Harry about.

"Harry you are going to have to say goodbye to your good, single buddy, me, next Saturday. I'm getting married. Now I know what you're gonna say, I've made two disastrous mistakes already, but this time it's different." Jimmy's happiness was reflected in his warm smile and steely blue eyes. His short cropped hair was reminiscent of his military service and he was of medium height and build, the picture of a man who worked out.

"Jimmy, you're the man! Hey I wouldn't dream of saying you shouldn't do it again. Maybe the third time will be the charm. Tell me about her."

"She's absolutely wonderful. Her name is Kathy. She has two really great kids. Before I met Kathy I never wanted kids, but these two are a pair of kids I really took to. Nicholas is a five year old boy and Robin is six, she's a girl. Kathy's widowed, her husband was killed in a car accident when they were on their way home from the hospital with the new baby. Can you imagine how awful that must have been?"

"It must have been terrible. I suppose now you want me to be your best man."

"Would you? And also I have a big favor to ask. Can we have a small reception afterwards, here at your place? I wouldn't want to impose but the wedding is just a small affair, not too many guests, and I haven't quite found a house yet. Her parents are in Europe and won't be able to get back in time for the wedding. I can't wait for you to meet Kathy and the kids."

"I'll be looking forward to it. And sure a reception here will be fine by me, but don't ask me to take the kids, I don't baby-sit." They high-fived each other and decided to go out and get some lunch. Jimmy had to look at a couple more houses but not for another hour or so. Later as Jimmy was leaving Harry added, "By the way congratulations and I'll see Saturday, at the church. Did you say ten a.m."

"No you ass, you know I said two p. m." Jimmy laughed.

"I know, see you then." He turned and walked through his door and as he closed it he thought, *Dumb ass you forgot to tell Jimmy about the peculiar frame. There's probably plenty of time for that and now I suppose I'd better see about renting a tux.*

The week flew by and Harry gave up on trying to accomplish writing anything. Practically every time he sat down to start the phone would ring and it would be Jimmy having second thoughts. Worrying about finding a decent house, would he make a good father? Was he good enough for Kathy? On and on. Harry calmed and reassured his friend and began to look forward to the wedding being over and done with. Jimmy and Kathy had ordered catered refreshments for a small gathering of twenty guests and Harry spent some hours cleaning out his refrigerator so all the extra food would fit. The wedding cake was to be delivered on the Friday before the wedding day and he spent some time moving the table next to a wall and rearranging furniture so there would be plenty of space for the guests to move around. Having only attended other peoples' weddings as a guest he had no idea that so much preparation was involved for such an event. *If I ever decide to take the plunge it will be an elopement, with no reception, no guests and I suppose if I think about it that way no woman would want to marry me!*

Saturday finally rolled around and Jimmy and Harry looked very handsome in their tuxes, the children very cute in their crisp, clean outfits, their sandy brown hair shone and had been brushed and slicked down with gel. Kathy looked very chic in a cream colored short-skirted satin suit. Her golden hair swept up on her head and covered by a short veil. The ceremony was over quite quickly and then the bride, groom and children and guests all made their way to Harry's house. A friend of Kathy's was going to take the children for a few days so she and Jimmy could go on a short honeymoon. Harry was glad about that as he knew that if asked to watch them he would have, but he didn't really want the responsibility. He had met them earlier in the week and found them to be quite nice children, but not enough to have them in his care.

The reception was going very well. The guests were having a great time over-indulging in food and champagne. Some of them had brought their children and after eating and standing around 'behaving themselves' they soon gravitated toward Nicholas and Robin. There were eight youngsters in all. After the initial name swapping the kids soon started a game of tag, running between guests and whooping and laughing when they were caught. Their loud laughs soon attracted the attention of their parents and they were told to go outside and continue their tag game in the small enclosed garden. When the adults realized that they no longer had to yell at each other to be heard over the noise from the children they broke up into small groups and quietly chatted and wished the new couple a long and happy life.

In the garden the children soon tired of the chasing game and little Nicholas threw himself down on the small patch of lawn and said to the other kids as they plopped down beside him,

"Lets play something else, I'm hot."

"There's nothing else to do here, and Mommy said we had to stay outside and not bother the grown-ups." Robin's serious little face was also flushed from running around as she said this to her younger brother.

"We could play 'I spy' that's a good quiet game." This was said by a little girl about the same age as Robin.

"I like 'I spy' what do you guys think?" Robin said with enthusiasm.

"I can't ever find a spy thing," whined Nicholas.

"Well how about hide-and-seek? We could be really, really quiet." The little girl who had suggested they play 'I spy' said. "We could hide inside and out and be very quiet if we hide in the house."

They all agreed hide-and-seek would be a fun thing to play. Robin agreed to be the first 'It' because she could count to two hundred if she had to but decided on just one hundred. She dutifully hid her eyes with her arms as she leaned against a small maple tree, kicking the trunk with her toes she counted. She counted slowly at first and could hear the other kids as they hid behind rustling bushes. Some of them were giggling and soon everything was quiet in the garden as each child found a good hiding spot. Robin counted to fifty and then speeded up the counting and when she reached eighty she skipped to ninety-nine and yelled, "Ready or not here I come!" The children weren't hard to find and when Robin found five of the children she had to look further afield for the last two, one of whom was her brother. She didn't want to stray too far from 'home' as the other two kids might get there before she found them and declare themselves 'safe.' After deciding that they must be hiding in the house Robin sighed, knowing that as soon as she entered the house the two missing kids would make a run for 'home.' As she was about to enter the house Harry came to the door and said,

"Anyone for cake?" It appeared that everyone was ready for cake even one of the not found kids who popped up out of an empty garbage can and joined the rest of the children as they charged toward the table holding the wedding cake. Harry toasted the happy couple as the kids jockeyed for a position closest to the bride while she and Jimmy sliced through the cake together. Neither one believed in cramming cake into each others faces so they just dropped pieces of the cake onto the wedding guest's plates. The children went back outside to eat theirs and the adults stood around congratulating the couple and complimenting them on a very pleasant reception.

Little Nicholas had been positively ecstatic when the game of hide-and-seek had been agreed on. Like most inquisitive children he had quickly scanned the inside of Harry's townhouse and made a mental note of things like where the bathroom was situated. He had scoped out the kitchen and checked the refrigerator to see where the ice and water dispensers were and unconsciously noticed that there was a closet near the front door.

When the game was decided on he immediately knew where he would hide and made his way there, muffling his delighted giggles with his little hands. He pretended he was an invisible boy and with his back to the wall he made his way through the house from the back door to the front door closet. Phew! He had made it without being seen, but of course that was because he was invisible. He tip-toed and reached up and opened the closet door. He backed into it and pulled the door closed behind him, no-one would find him here and he would win the game. Then he leaned against the side wall where the frame was positioned and to his horror found he was falling backwards. No one heard his shrieks of terror as he fell through the picture frame because everyone in the house was toasting the happy couple.

.6

It wasn't too long before Kathy noticed that Nicholas hadn't come to the table for his piece of cake. He loved cake and most certainly would have been first in line to get this piece if he knew it was being served. She went over to where Robin was sitting on the couch eating with some of the other children.

"Robin, honey, where's Nicholas?" she asked.

"I don't know Mommy. I haven't seen him since we played hide-and-seek. He must still be hiding and I forgot to find him."

"Well sweetie, go and look for him for Mommy after you finish your cake. There's a good girl."

Robin quickly cleaned up her plate and turned to the other children and asked,

"Anyone want to help me find my brother?" No one did so she took her empty plate out to the kitchen and went out the back door. She peeked behind bushes and even in the empty garbage can where one of the other kids had hidden. "Come out, come out where ever you are," she called, but received no giggles of delight from her little brother at his having been hidden so well. Her voice became more plaintive and louder as she received no answer to her call. "Don't worry you'll be safe and you win okay?" There was still no response from Nicholas. Robin began to lose her patience and resorted to a shrill scream that only little kids are capable of making. "Niiickiii, come out right now or you'll be in big trouble!" Of course there was no response from Nicholas but with all her shouting she had attracted the attention of the adults who wandered out of the house into the yard to see what all the noise was about. The children's mother and her new husband made a bee-line for Robin and demanded to know where Nicholas was. The poor kid was beginning to worry about her brother and broke out into tears and suggested that someone had kidnapped him. This was something that no-one wanted to even hear so they broke up into small groups and combed the back yard. When this didn't produce the little boy they went into the house and proceeded to search every nook and cranny and closet and still were unable to find him. Next they went out the front door thinking the child may have wandered off to explore the neighborhood, but how far could he have gone in the half hour or so that the cake had been cut and eaten?

Panic was starting to overtake Kathy and all Jimmy's soothing words did nothing to calm her.

"I'm calling the police right now." Harry said. "I'm sure by the time they get here the little guy will have turned up. Don't worry, I'm sure everything's all right." But Harry wasn't so sure. He had drank a lot of champagne and at the back of his mind his dulled senses couldn't quite put his finger on something that wasn't quite right in his house. He shook his head trying to clear it and think. "I'm going to put on a pot of fresh coffee," he said. He needed something to help his mind work faster. The local police only took a very short time to arrive and they agreed that the boy had probably wandered off and they would organize a search party to look for him. Meanwhile they put out an APB and an Amber Alert.

Jimmy went to their motel and found a photo of Nicholas in their luggage to give the police. While he was there he booked an extra night as it didn't look like they would leave on a honeymoon that day. He felt sure that by the time he got back to Harry's townhouse little Nicholas would be there being held in his Mom's arms. *This just can't be happening,* he thought. Then he got back in his car and headed back to Harry's and kept both his eyes wide open hoping to catch sight of a little lost boy.

Back at Harry's house there was no happy mother and child. Kathy was sobbing and clinging onto Robin as if she would never let her go. The police had taken statements from each of the wedding guests and let them go back to their own homes. They were told not to leave the area for the next forty-eight hours. The police told Kathy that there wasn't a whole lot they could do for the moment, and she and her daughter and husband could go back to their motel. Kathy was close to hysteria and said she wasn't going to move an inch until the police found Nicholas and returned him to her. Harry didn't blame her and told the couple he would be happy to have them stay the night.

"Can't you do something like bring in a K9 unit? I know a dog would find him right away." Kathy's voice shook with frustration and fear.

"Mommy I just know some evil people who wanted a little boy of their very own took Nicholas, kidnapped him, and now he will be someone else's little brother." Kathy's mouth dropped open, was this wishful thinking on Robin's part or did she actually see something? She grabbed her daughter by the shoulders and shook her like a rag doll.

"Did you see someone take him, Robin?" she screamed.

"No I didn't, but that's what I think happened to him, like in that movie we watched the other day." Now Robin's statement made sense and although Kathy was out of her mind with worry she made a mental note to be stricter about what the children watched from now on.

A K9 unit was on its way to Harry's house and so were several local television news teams. They arrived together and when Harry opened his door for what he thought was a special police unit he found himself inundated with questions and a microphone thrust into his face. Harry yelled,

"Get those fucking things out of my face will you! We're missing a kid here and you're not helping." Kathy was pushing herself through the throng of people crowding the front entrance to the house just as Jimmy pulled up and jumped out of his car.

"Honey did you find the photos of Nicholas?"
Enveloping Kathy in his arms he said he had and then added,

"I was hoping he'd be here." The lights shining on them from the camera men seemed very bright in the darkening evening light. A pushy news-woman with nicely coiffed golden hair a smart brown suit and very red lips shoved a microphone in their faces queried,

"Would you care to make a statement? Are you the parents of the missing boy?" Kathy had dissolved into tears and Jimmy said,

"Yes, this is his picture, he's only five years old and he just seems to have disappeared. Maybe you can run his picture on the news and ask if anyone has seen him."

The K9 unit had arrived with two handsome German Shepherds straining at their leashes. They were accompanied by a search and rescue team who quickly cordoned off the front of the townhouse and ushered the reporters out of the way so they could enter and leave the premises easily. Inside the house once more Kathy was holding Nicholas' little red windbreaker and the dog handlers were having the animals smell it. Once they were sure of the scent they wagged their tails furiously and one of the handlers said,

"We're good to go, we'll start in the back yard."

****

"Welcome to the six o' clock news, I'm Wes Wixey." The tanned, handsome news-anchor spoke straight into t.v. viewers' living rooms. He turned to his co-anchor and flashed a huge grin at her, displaying a mouth full of newly whitened teeth.

"And I'm Carla Carey," she flashed an equally bright set of overly white molars toward Will, they could have been siblings, and then turned back to the camera with the hint of a little frown on her brow, "Good evening. We have breaking news and an 'Amber alert' to start. But first these important messages." Their toothy white grins faded from the screen, leaving the impression of two

38

ghostly shadows of Cheshire cats and then they were replaced by commercials touting the merits of sleep-aids, followed by half a dozen side effects the aforementioned products might cause. After the advertisements the news anchors returned and their lead story was the disappearance of little Nicholas. His picture was flashed on the screen and Wes and Carla seriously exhorted their audience to contact the police if anyone had information about the little boy, or if they had seen anything suspicious in the neighborhood where the little boy had last been seen. They followed Nicholas' story with stories about gang-related shootings, traffic accidents and promises of the weather forecast if only their viewers would stay tuned. As the camera faded their images away they straightened the papers in front of them. If anyone knew what was written on those pages they carefully straightened each day, it would remain a mystery to viewers, because it was only obvious to anyone watching the broadcast that the anchors were reading the news from reader boards.

****

The police and dogs searched the back yard and then were dragged back into the house as the dogs kept their noses to the ground. Their sensitive sniffers picked up Nicholas' scent on the floor and wall all the way to the closet and when the police opened the door, it was empty and the dogs seemed to want to back away from it. Then they picked up the scent and it led to the front door and down the small path to the road, where they lost it. The handlers had the dogs go over the grounds and house again and the same thing happened. They concluded that maybe Robin was right someone had probably been driving past the townhouse and seen the little boy all by himself and abducted him. Kathy was inconsolable and Harry and Jimmy did their best to comfort her and convince her that the police knew their business and it would be no time at all before they found Nicholas. Eventually

Robin fell asleep on the couch and the three adults stayed up all night, sitting at the kitchen table drinking coffee and waiting for the phone to ring with good news about the boy. It didn't ring and periodically Kathy would pick it up to check for a dial tone.

7.

In his art studio Mark worked on another vast landscape, painted in oils in broad swaths of color. He was thinking about his life and how he had arrived at this moment in time. He was in his mid-thirties and had been an only child. He spent his childhood growing up in West Seattle with his parents who doted on him, as once they had reached their early fifties they had thought that they would end up being childless. They had not named him Mark Down, his name was Johnny Brown. Being adored by his parents and what they thought of as their miracle baby he was never denied anything while growing up. Although giving their son whatever he wanted made the parents feel good, it only made Mark a selfish person with a sense of entitlement. He didn't mix easily with other children and spent most of his first years in school watching the other children play together. When he did join in their childish games he expected to get his way and if he didn't win in a game of tag he would sulk and go off to be alone. It was the same through his high school years, if he couldn't be the star of the team he didn't want to play.

The day after Mark graduated from high school his parents were in a shopping mall and were the victims of a random shooting. At eighteen Mark was alone with no parents and very few friends. Some distant relatives, ones he didn't know, sent notes of regret and consolation and hoped he would remember his parents with love and affection. He didn't know how these people knew about his parents' demise or why they wrote to him. As far as remembering his parents with love, up to this point in his life, Mark only loved himself, he crumpled the notes and cards and tossed them in the garbage. He inherited his parents' home, savings accounts, stocks and vehicles. He figured he didn't need to go to college because at an early age his parents had practically swooned at his artistic abilities. He would be an artist and sell his pictures for big bucks. Life would be a snap.

Life turned out not to be a snap. Gallery owners seemed not to like him so didn't consider showing his oils. Worse it occurred to him one day that every interaction with prospective buyers ended up with him arguing with gallery owners, and him stomping out the door, pictures under his arm and invectives spewing from his mouth. Nobody liked him and why would they with a name like Johnny Brown! He decided to change it, and his attitude along with his name. He'd show the world what a great artist and person he was. After this decision was made, things began to fall into place for him. He found his new name in a supermarket. While he was filling his cart with steaks and frozen potato bites he overheard a middle aged woman talking to her friend.

"Look Maggie, there's a marked down cart. I love anything that has a 'mark down' label on it." Since Mark was looking for a new name, this one seemed to really fill the bill so he became Mark Down, who wouldn't love him with a name like that? He also thought a lot about being liked. It didn't take an idiot to tell him he rubbed people the wrong way. He went to a book store and found a book titled, 'How to be liked by Every-one, for Dummies.' He bought it and read it from cover to cover. He thought the suggestions in the text to be a lot of bullshit. He still adhered to a mindset that was, everyone should love him, as his parents had, but he didn't have to love or be nice in return. He did slowly begin to be respectful of the local art gallery owners but with most other people he was brusque, bordering on rude.

M ark had an excellent eye for choosing and m ixing his colors and pored over volum e after volum e of pictures by the m asters and realized that he needed to see som e of these works for him self. He had his law yer rent out his house for him as he didn't want it left empty, and decided to go to France, Italy and Spain and m aybe England for a year and hope that he could absorb som e of their techniques by osm osis. It was a good m ove for him , as it not only im proved his eye for art, but w hen he had to interact w ith people w ho spoke foreign languages he had to be patient with them or they wouldn't put up with his temperamental outbursts. He even found that he had a knack for learning different languages. H is year stretched into two and during this tim e he had a steam y affair w ith a french art student but she didn't want to marry him . This w as a big blow to his ego. He selfishly vow ed to never fall in love again and w ent across the English Channel and fell in love w ith the English countryside. The rolling hills and checkerboard fields w ere a landscape artist's dream come true. He spent six months there and when he found him self becom ing attracted to a local barm aid he decided he didn't want to be hurt again and bought an air ticket to N ew Y ork.

Once in New York he did all the touristy things, visiting the museums, the opera, Broadway and checked out a local artist's commune. It was there that he finally felt he had found a place and people who understood him, and he them. He rented a small, cramped and somewhat grubby loft apartment. He started painting large canvases of scenes he had seen over the past couple of years and found that for the first time ever he felt content, happy even. He even fell in love again. Her name was Bethany. She was short, black haired and slender with eyes that looked like pools of ebony and Mark decided if he had to die then he wouldn't mind drowning in those pools. She was vivacious and gregarious and wasn't afraid to be affectionate either in private or public. She was very good for Mark and it seemed Mark was good for her. She made silver and copper jewelry.

One morning, after a late night of partying with a group of artists, Bethany rolled out of Mark's rumpled single bed and stretched. Mark was watching her and thought her the most beautiful thing in the world.

"Mark do you think an artist has to suffer in order to be great?"

"Come back to bed, I think artists should do things that make them happy. It would make me happy if you came back to bed." He lifted the covers invitingly.

"I'm serious. Coffee I need coffee." She walked the few steps it took to reach a hot-plate and coffee pot. She measured the coffee grounds and plugged the pot into the electric outlet. She twirled her long black hair into a knot and looked around for something to secure it with. One of Mark's slender paint brushes was handy so she used that. "It seems to me that all the great artists have suffered. I'm thinking I won't be great until I've suffered some awful tragedy. Have you suffered a lot of stuff Mark? Because I think you are a really great artist. Your landscapes are magnificent, so you must have suffered a lot"

"Well I'm sure suffering now. Are you coming back to bed?"

"It's almost one 'o clock. Get up." Mark pulled the covers over his head and heard Bethany turn on the shower, the noise of the coffee percolating and the sound of Bethany singing, 'They paved Paradise and put in a parking lot. Don't it always seem to be that you don't know what you've got 'til it's gone, they paved paradise and put in a parking lot.' It was an old sixties song that had made a comeback, but with a new singer. These sounds lulled Mark into a slumber and he was jerked awake when Bethany pulled the covers from his head and kissed his cheek. He grabbed for her and she said,

'Maybe later. Get up, I made pancakes, and after we eat I think we should go on an adventure." Mark turned over and was about to go back to sleep, but Bethany was way ahead of him and yanked the covers off him. So he gave up on sleep and they ate pancakes, drank coffee and eventually Mark ended up dressed and ready for Bethany's adventure. She was very impulsive and he hoped she wouldn't do anything to embarrass him.

It was close to three before they actually started out on their adventure. The weather was breezy and low clouds scudded across the sky. They wore light jackets and scarves, held hands as they walked down the streets.

"This is nice, but hardly an adventure." Mark was smiling down at her with loving eyes. She looked up at him and laughed.

"Well it soon will be. I've decided that I don't want to exactly suffer myself so I thought we could come out here and watch other people suffer."

"You know Bethany sometimes I think you are a bit weird. What makes you want to see someone suffer?"

"I think it will make me a better artist." They walked the back streets of the city and eventually they came across a soup kitchen. The sign outside said 'All are welcome. If you are hungry we will feed you. If you've lost your soul we will find it for you." The couple stopped in front of this sign and Bethany let go of Marks hand and hugged herself.

"This is it. We'll find suffering people inside. Come on let's go in." Bethany pulled on Mark's arm and steered him through the doorway.

"Are you sure we should go inside? We don't need to be fed or find our souls." Mark knew saying this would do absolutely no good. It was impossible to change Bethany's mind once she had decided to do something. Once they entered the soup kitchen they saw a room that wasn't all that big. There was room for several large tables with salt and pepper shakers and bottles of ketchup on them. There was a hatch in the wall where presumably you would be passed a meal. There were several scruffy looking old men seated at one of the tables and a family of six was seated at the other, a mother and father and four kids from about two years old to about ten. All had plates of steaming food. It looked to be a filling meal of cabbage, mashed potatoes and meat loaf. Dragging Mark behind her Bethany sat them down at one of the tables. Bethany smiled brightly as all eyes in the room turned to stare at them. One of the scruffy men said,

"Ya gotta go up to the hatch to get yer meal. Ain't got no table service in here."

Mark stood and pulled on Bethany's hand and tried to head toward the door but Bethany had other ideas and pulled him toward the hatch.

"Please don't do this. We don't need to eat here and these people don't look like they are suffering." Mark said in a hushed voice. A face appeared in the hatch space. It was a big burly guy wearing a chef's hat and a white priest's collar. His short sleeves revealed arms covered with maritime tattoos He grinned at them and in a booming voice said,

"Welcome. Did you come for a bite to eat , or for some soul food?" It was hard not to grin back at him as the m an exuded an aura of good w ill and a zest for life . M ark could have disappeared into the ground as B ethany brightly replied .

"No food thanks Rev. we just came to observe suffering people."

"Well little girly you came to the wrong p lace for that. Look around you, these folks aren't suffering and that's because in here we ease the pain out of both body and soul." M ark w as feeling distinctly uncom fortable and as he grabbed Bethany's hand he muttered apologies for having bothered the Reverend and dragged her outside .

"Why did you do that?" Bethany was giggling at Mark's obvious discom fort.

"Because I'm a bit mystified by your behavior, that's why."

"Well I'm just trying to find out what it's like to suffer that's all.

They w alked for another half hour in silence . The streets w ere filled w ith busy shoppers and sm elly alleyw ays, restaurants and shops. O n the side street of a deli w as a dum pster and M ark noticed the head of a m an pop up out of it. H e nudged B ethany and said,

"Now if you w ant to see suffering look at that guy, he is probably suffering, don't you think?"

"This is great, let's go down the alley -w ays instead of the m ain street. I should have thought of that before. Mark you're the best." She reached up and gave him a peck on the cheek . The alleyw ays w ere for the m ost part dirty and stinking w ith dum psters overflow ing w ith garbage and hom eless people lounging in paper boxes or little encam pm ents in recesses in som e of the w alls.

"Now this is what I call an adventure. These people look like they are needy and they are positively oozing with pain and suffering."

"You don't know that. Maybe this is how they like to live. Maybe they are happy."

"Are you happy?" Bethany stopped and asked a man dressed in rags and holding a bottle in a brown paper sack and leaning against a brick wall. His face was unshaven and his beard displayed the remnants of countless meals. He opened a toothless mouth and opened his arms as if to embrace Bethany. Out of his mouth wafted a stench that almost overpowered both Bethany and Mark. Mark grabbed Bethany and dragged her toward the exit of the alley. Bethany seemed to be enjoying herself because she was quietly giggling as she was being pulled along.

"Beth I think we have seen enough of the sufferers, let's go home before you make me suffer any more in these alleyways. She agreed and they started toward home. At the end of the alleyway was a long dumpster with lots of broken furniture in it. On the side of it was a sign that said 'Recycle your old furniture for free.'

"Look at all these neat pieces of wood and junk. I bet we could find all kinds of treasures in this dumpster." Bethany's enthusiasm for weird stuff never ceased to amuse Mark.

"We don't need any of that stuff. It's late we should be getting back and I'm hungry." Just as Mark was thinking that he would have to drag her away from the dumpster a wild-eyed woman with disheveled grey hair and a ragged coat walked up to the dumpster and threw a large empty picture frame on top of the pile.

"You rotten bastard, I hate you for leaving me," she screamed, "well now I'm leaving you, and putting you in the trash where you belong." Her face was streaming with tears and she turned and with surprising speed ran off down the alley.

"Now that was real suffering if ever I saw it. Mark we have to get that picture frame out of there and take it home. It will be my inspiration." Mark climbed into the dumpster and said, "We, meaning me?" as he retrieved the frame thinking, *the things I do for that woman. I'll probably have to ask her to marry me because the only explanation for my behavior is that I love her.* The realization left him with a feeling of euphoria and the walk back to the apartment was like walking on air.

8.

Harry was exhausted. The past couple of weeks had been a nightmare with search parties combing the house and neighborhood for any signs of who had abducted little Nicholas. Jimmy and Kathy, with a bit of help from Harry, had come up with a $25,000 reward for anyone giving them information leading to the recovery of the child. But after two weeks of no-one offering any information or help at all, the outlook didn't seem good. Kathy was starting to look like a shadow of her former self. She wasn't eating or taking care of herself or Robin. The little grieving family was still at Harry's house and the situation was beginning to wear Harry down. He felt a huge sense of responsibility for what had happened but he didn't know what to do about it any more. He talked to Jimmy and the two men set out to seriously look at properties for sale as close to Harry as possible. They found one about a block away and quietly closed the deal and moved Kathy's and Jimmy's household goods into it.

On a crisp autumn morning with the colored leaves floating to the ground, Jimmy and Kathy sat at Harry's kitchen table drinking coffee, looking out the window as they fell. Jimmy said,

"Honey I want you and Robin to shower and get dressed and I have something to show you, okay?"

"They've found Nicholas haven't they, and he's dead isn't he?" Her face crumpled and tears fell once again. As Jimmy looked at her he felt his heart might break. But he pushed on, making his voice sound confident.

"No it's nothing like that! I have a little surprise for my two best girls." He hoped beyond hope that she would start to move forward once she saw how nicely he and Harry had set up the house. Although it was a tough decision, after they had consulted with a grief counselor, they had moved Nicholas' things into a nicely decorated boy's bedroom complete with his toys, model airplanes and dinosaurs. Robin's room was equally charming and the master bedroom was a bit bare except for a bed. Jimmy hoped that getting things for the house might help Kathy recover, and poor little Robin needed to get into a school instead of moping around with her mother all day long.

The drive over to the new house only took minutes and Jimmy hoped this would add some relief for Kathy as she could just pop over to Harry's house to see if Nicholas had turned up. He was pretty sure this would be comforting to her as he knew she would probably take a long time to accept that he was gone. What a nasty burden she had to bear, it was almost certain to be bringing back memories of the loss of her first husband. It was hard for Jimmy as well because he had grown to like the little guy.

"Well girls here we are. Welcome to our new home." Robin perked up as they walked down the little path to a townhouse very similar to Harry's. Kathy could just as well have been a zombie from a horror movie.

"This is our house?" she asked in a flat unemotional tone. Jimmy unlocked the front door and ushered them in. They looked into every room and when they came to Robin's room the child smiled with delight at seeing her belongings and toys. She jumped on the bed and hugged some of her dolls and Beanie babies. Kathy flatly stated the master bedroom needed more furniture a dressing table and a couple of chest of drawers. Jimmy agreed and then led her to Nicholas' room.

"For when we find him, it will all be ready for him." He said this as he patted her shoulder and then she sat on the little bed, picked up a worn but loved teddy, buried her nose in it and sobbed as if her heart would never mend. Robin stared at her mother and tears rose in her eyes also, but Jimmy put his arms around her and said, "Lets leave Mommy here for a bit, we'll make some hot chocolate." He gently led her from the room and quietly closed the door behind them. They went to the kitchen where he heated milk and hoped that he had done the right thing. He simply didn't know what else he could do for her.

After they left Harry threw himself down on the couch and breathed a ragged sigh. He was pleased to have the house back to himself but wished it could have been under better circumstances. He had been unable to write with his friend and family being a constant reminder of the kid's disappearance and thought it would help him a lot if he got back to it. Also he hadn't jogged the whole time they were there and so his first thought was that a good run would clear his head and while doing so he would decide what to write next in his 'Great American Exposé.'

The cool air and beautiful fall colors of the leaves were exactly what Harry had needed. He began to feel a lot better. The huge breaths that he took filled his lungs with fresh air and made him feel a bit dizzy, like a non-smoker taking a huge drag from a cigarette.

When he left his house he had headed in the direction of his friend's place but after he had ran half the distance to it, he thought he needed to steer clear of them for a while. Being with them was too emotionally draining so he jogged in place for a minute and turned and jogged in the opposite direction. He was surprised at how quickly he had gotten out of shape, it wasn't long before he became winded and his legs were tiring. He could barely manage a 'Mornin, to your left,' as he trotted along passing other pedestrians. When he thought he had jogged far enough, he decided to go for just one more block and then turn around and go back.

At the end of the block he could see a lamp post with what looked like a wanted-poster tacked to it. He wished he hadn't gone that far when he got there. It wasn't a wanted-poster it was a picture of Nicholas and under his smiling face a sentence read, 'Have you seen me? My name is Nicholas and my Mommy and Daddy want me back." Harry turned around and pounded the pavement with speedy steps until he arrived back at his house, out of breath and with tears running down his face, from either the chilly air or the wave of sickening sadness that had overwhelmed him, when he had read the poster.

Harry had taken a shower after he got home and then sat in front of his computer, his hands poised above the keys and not a single sentence flowed from his fingers and onto the blank page. He needed to keep busy so he sat at the other computer and went onto a game site and bought half a dozen games. It didn't take long to download them and he spent a good part of the day playing some familiar games like scrabble, and trying out some games he had never played before. The game playing was good for him he had spent several hours without thinking at all about sad things, missing children, lost pets or even the sorry conditions of the people he had met while in Iraq.

When Harry was tired of playing games and knew he wasn't ready to continue his writing he left the computer room, sat in front of the television and flipped channels until he came to a channel featuring chefs and how to barbecue. One of the chefs was even offering plans on how to build an outdoor barbecue pit. By God, *that's what you need Harry, a* barbecue! So he called the number on the screen and bought the plans, and paid for them with a credit card.

The plans arrived by overnight delivery and after Harry opened them and scanned the list of supplies he would need. He went to his small back yard and measured out where the pit would be. He got a shovel from a small shed, pulled off his shirt and started to dig the hole. The weather was cool but it wasn't long before Harry had worked up a good sweat. He stood to wipe his forehead with the back of his hand, as he did so he noticed a nice looking woman watching him out of an open window from the house next door to him. He smiled and waved and she waved back.

"What are you digging that hole for, a fish pond?" she asked as she poked her head out of the window, a slight breeze blew her chin level brown hair into her mouth as she spoke. She pulled it out in a practiced way as if it happened all the time.

"No, it's for a barbecue pit. Maybe after I'm done I'll have you and your husband over for hamburgers. By the way I'm Harry, Harry Prentice."

With twinkling blue eyes and an amused smile the neighbor replied, "My name's Alice, and there is no husband. I'm divorced and available. Anyway what happened to the little kid that went missing from your place?" Harry groaned, and he just told her he really didn't know. Did I hear right, she actually said she is available. What a strange expression. Was she advertising herself?

"It's nice to meet you Alice. And I am also available. Maybe we could have a drink together sometime." He wasn't sure about this, but the truth was that he wasn't getting any younger and in spite of Jimmy's unfortunate experience with Nicholas and all that entailed, Harry had been a bit envious of his friend's new relationship.

"Why not? Maybe this weekend we could get together. I work four ten hour days and then three off, so I'm pretty tired in the week."

"Well I'm retired, so I can do anything anytime. Where do you work?"

"You don't look old enough to retire." Alice said tilting her head and looking at him as if trying to figure out how old he was. "Hang on a minute I'm coming out, I can't hear you very well."

Her head disappeared and she reappeared carrying a glass of iced lemonade in each hand. She leaned over the short hedge separating the small back yards and handed him one of the glasses, displaying voluptuous breasts barely covered by a low cut blouse, and said, "Nice to meet you Harry." Harry drained the glass and said,

"Well if I want to finish this I'd better get back to it. How about we grab a beer, on say Saturday night? About eight?" She nodded and breathlessly agreed. She turned and went to her house with an exaggerated swing of her hips. Harry whistled while he worked at digging his hole. On the way to the local hardware store he thought, If we hate each other it will be very uncomfortable living right next door to *each other. I think I'd best* go really slow with her, but she sure is a looker!

9.

Detective Roger Brown sat with his feet propped up on his desk, the chair tilted at a dangerous angle as he ever so carefully rocked back and forth. Every now and then Angela would pop her happy little face around the door and ask him if he needed anything. He would smile to himself and wonder had he ever been that eager and full of energy when he was her age? He supposed it was a youthful disease that he had recovered from.

He shuffled through the many pages of missing people and felt a slight depression envelope him as he realized that the majority of these cases were never satisfactorily solved. Where did all those people go to? Maybe there was a secret door they all went through, and then lived happily ever after, when they walked through it. Well he guessed a fairy tale like that was better than the reality of them being murdered, abducted or worse.

Angela tapped on his door at noon and handed him a bag from Burger King with a number five chicken sandwich, fries and a cup of atrocious coffee in a stiff cardboard cup.

" I'm off this afternoon, but I thought this was so interesting that I'd give it to you today rather than in the morning." She proffered a file containing information about missing children in the area.

"Angela, you know we don't do kids, that's another department."

"I know but look at the address and see if it doesn't ring a bell. 'Gotta go. I have a date with my beautician." She breezed out of his office, failing to close the door behind her.

Roger flipped the file open as he reached in the burger bag for a handful of fries. Then he emptied the contents onto his desk and looked for the packets of ketchup. He was just about to take a bite of his burger when he found himself looking at a picture of a cute little boy smiling at him with one front tooth missing and a little white line of new enamel where a new tooth was sprouting. It was a picture of Nicholas. He looked at the address and groaned and thought, *There's something rotten in Denmark!*

An hour later Roger was standing at Harry's front door ringing the bell and hoping the new owner was at home. A breeze had picked up and was blowing his hair every which way and was seeping right through his light jacket. *It won't be long before winter gets here. People don't go missing as much in winter. Makes my job easier.*

He was just about to ring the bell a second time when the door opened and Harry, wearing a jogging suit, opened the door and raised one eye quizzically.

"Yes?" Roger withdrew the picture of Nicholas and held it in front of Harry.

"You'd better come in." said Harry with a sick feeling in the pit of his stomach. "Have you found the little guy? Please don't tell me he's dead." Roger sensed the deep sadness Harry was feeling and wished life wasn't so hard sometimes. He introduced himself and asked if Harry was aware of the previous disappearances from this house.

"Yes Officer Brown, I had heard about them from the real estate woman. I can hardly believe they are related, unless someone has it in for the residents of this house."

"Just call me Roger. They might be related and that's why I wanted to talk to you. I know you have been interviewed about the kid and there's no way you are suspect in any way. We also know that you weren't even in the country when the other three went missing, so I guess what I'm getting at is the possibility that you could disappear."

"Christ," Harry said running his hands over his unshaven stubble. He had planned to shave after he jogged but had sat down and started writing and lost track of time. He noticed he was hungry, he hadn't eaten either. "Let's go in the kitchen and get some coffee. I'm going to fix me a sandwich, can I make one for you?"

"No thanks, I already ate, but coffee sounds good." As Harry plugged the coffee-pot into the outlet he pulled two cups from the cupboard and a plate for his sandwich. He needed to go shopping so he settled on peanut butter and jelly as there wasn't much else.

"If someone has it in for the occupants of this house, logically you would be the next victim. Would you be agreeable to our department setting up some surveillance equipment in and around the exterior of your house."

"Well that's mighty good of you. I have to admit this is a total surprise, because that kind of stuff would cost your department a pretty penny. I don't think it's needed though. I've been in combat several times and worked the routes between camps in Iraq. I can take care of myself."

"Well Mr. Prentice I hope you will understand how important this is. Four people from this exact location are cause for a great deal of speculation." He took the cup of coffee that Harry had pushed toward him. It's not entirely just for your protection, it might help us solve this very difficult case. We have several families out there who are devastated. If we could come up with an explanation for them it would go a long way towards them getting some closure, then they could move on with their lives." Harry felt a bit ashamed. He must have sounded very selfish.

"Well since you put it that way I do understand. Go ahead and with my blessing. If there's anything I can do to help, just say so."

"Thank you Mr. Prentice."

"Call me Harry."

"Sure thing, Harry. Could we get started on this first thing in the morning?"

"Be my guests, I'll be sure to be up and dressed." After a few pleasantries Roger left. Harry's mind was racing with possibilities of how these disappearances impacted him. He thought physical activities would be better than writing so he went out to his back yard to work on the barbecue. It was almost finished and he was very pleased with his handiwork. He would let the cement dry for a couple of days and then fire the thing up.

Back in his office Roger wrote up a report on how Harry had been co-operative and agreed to the surveillance of his home. Roger made a note to himself to thank Angela for bringing the boy's disappearance to his attention. She was turning out to be a big asset to him. He hoped this tactic of surveillance would turn up some evidence to help solve these seemingly unsolvable cases. So far there had been absolutely no clues, nothing to give them even a hint as to what had happened to these people. It was particularly disturbing when the child had gone missing from that house.

****

Nicholas was walking around in a semi-dark place. He couldn't see anything clearly, there didn't seem to be any other kids or people around, just shadows that would flit past him so quickly he wasn't sure if they were real or not. His thin voice wavered as he walked with his hands outstretched in front of him. "Mommy where are you?" He wailed. No one answered him, so he just kept walking forwards.

10.

When Mark and Bethany got back to the apartment they were out of breath and invigorated after their 'adventure.' They were also ravenously hungry and after tossing the picture frame in a corner of the room, already stacked with empty ready-made frames, they washed their hands and faces and went out to a local pizza house to eat. It was a little way around the corner from where they lived and when they entered, the smell of baking pizza dough was like a place in heaven. Their mouths watered in anticipation of a fresh baked Hawaiian smothered in cheese and pineapples.

"We should go on more adventures. That one really was a lot of fun." Bethany said with a mouthful of pizza that dripped tomato sauce out of the corner of her mouth.

"You look like a vampire," Mark said as he leaned across the table and wiped her mouth clean with his napkin.

A group of their friends bustled themselves into the pizza place and after asking if it was okay, they sat at the same table as Mark and Bethany.

"Mark tell the guys about our adventure today. You won't believe what happened. We found the neatest old picture frame in a dumpster. An insane woman tossed it in there and she was screaming at it as she did so. Tell them Mark."

Smiling indulgently he said, "It sounds like you already did!" Their friends didn't think it sounded like a real adventure but they chatted together and ordered more pizza and beers and finally left after midnight. "I'm beat Beth, let's call it a night." Mark pulled Bethany out of her seat and with their arms around each other they walked the short distance home and fell into bed and into a fitful sleep.

When Mark woke up the next morning it was to find that Bethany was no longer snuggled up against him. All the lights were on in the tiny apartment and Mark pulled covers over his eyes to shade them from the glare. Once Bethany was up she liked Mark to get up as well, so it was no surprise to him when he felt the covers yanked out of his clutching fingers. She was still in her p.j.s as she bent and kissed him, with her voice quivering with excitement she said,

"Mark, I just discovered the coolest thing about that old frame we found."

"You don't say. It's so tacky looking the old woman was probably doing the world a favor by junking it."

"You won't think that when I show you what it can do. Come on and get up and I'll show you." Mark knew it was useless to try and argue so he rolled out of bed and pulled on his pants and a ratty old sweater. It was his favorite because Bethany had found it at a second hand store and given it to him. He had never told her that he could afford to shop at exclusive men's clothing stores. He planned to share that information with her after they were married. He had to ask her first and he was pretty sure she would say yes. Maybe this evening he would do just that.

"Okay I'm up. Show me what," he made air quotes with his fingers, "it can do."

"Prepare to be amazed and astonished." Bethany had leaned the frame against the wall and stood next to it. It was as high as her waist. "Does this frame look unusual to you in any way?" She asked Mark. He had his arms folded and his head tilted to one side and slowly a frown formed on his brow.

"It looks pretty normal to me. It's not even that great looking. I'm thinking I would never use it for one of my works."

"Well look at this!" Bethany thrust her arm into frame and instead of it being stopped by the wall behind it, it just disappeared.

Mark burst out laughing and said, "Good one Bethany. Planning to be an illusionist are we?"

"Now watch this." Bethany went to the table and plucked a handful of grapes from a fruit bowl. One by one she tossed them at the frame and they all seemed to disappear.

"That is pretty impressive, what's the trick?" Mark was grinning from ear to ear and feeling quite proud of her expertise.

"It's not a trick! I think this frame has magical properties."

"Honey, let's get real here, there's no such thing as magic. It's an optical illusion. Just tell me how you do it." Bethany picked the frame from against the wall and after clearing a space on the floor she put it down and asked Mark,

"Now do you see anything unusual about this frame?"

"Nope, can't say that I do. Why don't you just tell me what is unusual about it"

"Doesn't it seem odd to you that you can't see the floor through the frame?" Mark stepped forward to take a closer look. "Now that you mention it, that is kind of odd," For some reason Mark was overcome by a feeling of unease, the blood seemed to drain from his head down to his feet. Bethany was standing next to it and began to chant, "I can put my foot in, and I can pull my foot out." Each time she did so she sang along. Mark said,

"Be careful, you don't know what might happen."

He was curious about the seemingly impossible notion that there was a cavity in the frame. By way of proving it to himself he picked up a stack of books he had planned on giving away. He held one over the frame and let it go. It fell as far as the frame and then it was gone. The other books followed, but they couldn't hear them land.

"Maybe we should take it to the police and see what they think." Mark sounded very serious, if not a tad scared.

"No way! They would never give it back to us." Bethany sounded outraged. "It's ours and I think we should keep it. I have to go to the studio and finish up some bracelets and earrings and a few other things that have been on special order. Promise you won't do anything with it while I'm gone." She started to peel off her pajamas on her way to the shower. Mark watched her shaking his head. Bethany turned to him and with a sweet smile she said, "Promise?" How could he resist her and so he nodded his head and leaned the frame back against the wall before plugging in the coffee-pot and putting bread in the toaster.

After Bethany had left to go and work on her jewelry, Mark knew that he would never be able to concentrate enough to work on either of a couple of canvases he was in the middle of painting. He stood in front of the frame and cautiously pushed his hand in and pulled it out. Then he looked around the apartment to see what else he could toss in there. He opened up the one coat closet in the place and pulled out some old smelly sneakers that had seen better days, so he tossed them in. Gone! Great! He looked around for something else and since the sink was piled high with dirty dishes they went in as well. Mark really began to get into what he was doing and in a short time the apartment was looking quite bare. He tossed in anything he thought he could easily replace and soon the only things left were the bed, a couple of chairs, the bed clothes, toaster and electric kettle and his paintings and easels, and Bethany's clothes. He didn't think she would be thrilled if he tossed those. When the tossing ceased to be fun he poked his head through the space and yelled,

"Is anyone in here? Can anyone hear me?" His questions went unanswered and his face was brushed by a slight breeze and held the hint of smelly sneakers on it. It wasn't exactly dark in there but not light enough for him to make out any objects. He straightened up and had a brilliant idea. I need a long piece of rope and a big hook. Maybe I can hook something and pull it out. I wonder how far down it goes. Almost as quickly as he had the thought he pulled on a jacket, checked his wallet and put it in the back pocket of his pants, then left the apartment for a local hardware store. At the store he bought a length of thick rope measuring two hundred feet long. He thought that was probably overkill but then there wasn't any way he could guess what length he would need. He also bought a big, heavy hook.

"You must be fishing for something really big!" The salesman joked as Mark paid for the items.

"One can only hope." He responded, thinking maybe he shouldn't have tossed in those last couple of chairs, they hadn't been in that bad of a condition. If he was lucky maybe he could get them back out. He didn't say that to the salesman because even to him the idea of fishing things out of a picture frame sounded utterly insane.

Once back in the apartment Mark sat on the floor and set about attaching the hook to the rope. When that was done he tied the end of the rope without the hook to the leg of the bed, placed the frame flat on the floor and tossed the hook into the frame. The whole length of rope sailed over the edge of the frame and dangled in the emptiness. Stretched out on his stomach he reached his arm into the void and grabbed the rope and began to swing the rope back and forth like a pendulum. It was difficult to say if he was snagging anything. If he did he thought that there would be a sound to indicate the hook touching something, or the weight of the rope would change. He kept up the swinging motion for a good ten minutes until his arm ached, then began to reel the rope back into the room. He hadn't caught anything and was a bit disappointed. He reheated the morning coffee and made a sandwich. There were no plates to put it on, so he used a paper towel in place of a plate. He was pleased that he hadn't emptied the drawer where he kept the silverware into the frame. When he had eaten he tossed the faux napkin into the hole. *Maybe this thing isn't so bad after all. It makes a great garbage disposal, everybody ought to have one.*

Bethany was only gone for about four hours but when she returned, her eyes roamed around the apartment and it looked a lot less cluttered than when she had left. With a little smile playing at the corners of her lips she placed her hands on her hips and said,

"What have you been up to, having fun with the frame are we?"

"I may have got a bit carried away."

"Well I hope you can get some of that stuff back out of there. From where I'm standing it looks like we might have to go buy some new dishes. Or, now here's a silly thought, did you wash the dishes and put them away?" She would have bet money that he hadn't. She let out peals of laughter and added, "Now admit it, this is the best thing that has ever happened to us." She sat down cross legged next to the frame, rested her head on her hands and stared into it. Mark stood behind her with his hands on her shoulders and also stared into the strange empty space.

11

Harry had been correct to be cautious about dating his next-door neighbor, Alice. She was pretty and very pleasant, and also what he thought of as clingy. She possibly was an affectionate type of person and Harry could be affectionate too, but not after just a couple of dates. On their first date, if you could call it that, it was just having a beer together and eating bar hors d'ouvres. She was very chatty, it could have been she was nervous, but she actually never stopped talking. Harry felt that he now knew her whole life history. All her likes and dislikes, she had never given him a chance to talk, or even asked him about himself. That was okay with him on the first date but on the second and third dates she was the same. The only thing that she was curious about was the fact that he lived in a house that was becoming notorious for people disappearing from it. Since it was as much a mystery to him as it was to the investigating detectives he didn't feel that he wanted to talk to her about it. She worked for a collection agency and talked a lot about her job.

"Honestly Harry you wouldn't believe how rude some people can be. Sometimes they hang up before I can tell them who I am." Harry raised an eyebrow as he looked at her across the table of a booth they were sitting in, at a Chinese restaurant.

Come on Harry just tell her that you really can't stand to eat with her one more time. Tell her she's a motor mouth. Tell her she is boring. Tell her anything so you can get out of here. Alice took the raised eyebrow to mean Harry was sitting on the edge of his seat waiting to hear the rest of her story.

"It's true, I mean they must have a sixth sense that the call is from a collection agency. So, most of the time, I don't even say who the call is from when they answer. I just start my pitch. It's not my fault they don't pay their bills." Harry sighed and motioned the waiter to bring the bill. "Sometimes they even swear at me. Can you believe that?"

Can and do. I don't even blame them! I feel like swearing at you myself.

"Come on Alice, it's time I was getting back. I want to check to see if the bars in my barbecue have set. When they do I'll be all ready to fix hot dogs whenever I want some."

Alice fussily checked her lipstick and then she raised her hand to catch the attention of the waiter and asked for a foam box for her leftovers. They drove the short distance from the restaurant to their homes, not in silence, as Harry would have liked, but to the sounds of Alice droning on about the most inconsequential matters. How could anyone who looked so cute be so full of herself and think it was okay to be that way. They pulled up in front of Harry's place and he got out of the car and opened the door for her.

"Want to come in my house for a nightcap," Alice asked as she reached to grasp Harry's hand. Harry side-stepped away from her and shoved his hands in his pants pockets.

"Look Alice, this is so hard to say. It's not you it's..

"IT'S ME!" she shrieked at him. "Like I'm an idiot and don't know what's happening here. Why did you keep asking me out if you were going to drop me like this. You jerks are all the same."

"I'm so sorry I didn't want this to happen. And you know, it was you who kept asking me to go out, after that first time. We can still be friends and we are already neighbors."

"Friends with you! You know what you can do with your friendship? Shove it up your ass. You jerk, with neighbors like you, who needs enemies?" She turned, and stiff backed, strutted to her front door and after she opened it and went into her house she slammed it shut. Then just to let Harry know how upset she was she opened it again and screamed, "I hope you go to hell you rat-bastard." She slammed it shut a second time and Harry felt horrible. He thought it was a good thing that he hadn't been going out with her any longer than he had. What would her reaction have been like then?

After Harry got in his house he lost his jacket and went out to check to see if his barbecue cement had dried. He also wondered if the surveillance cameras had caught her little outburst. The cement was perfect and so he bent to lift the metal cover for the grill and attach it to the base, as he did so he noticed Alice yank her drapes closed so she could not see him. *She'll get over it. God only knows I have.*

But she wasn't over it yet, and Alice sat on her couch and plotted revenge. *He's the last guy I'm going to let put one over on me again! Those bastards I've had it with them. Who needs them? I don't.* She didn't have an immediate plan but was sure she would know when the right opportunity presented itself.

A few days later Harry was on a hot streak with his novel and realized that he had sat over his computer keyboard for over four hours. He needed a break so he stood and stretched and bent and touched his toes. He had thought to give Alice a call a couple of times, to see if she was okay, but hadn't in case she thought he was trying to go out with her again; the last thing on his mind. He did pick up the phone and call Jimmy. There was no answer and he left a message asking his friend to call him back. He also added that he would like to have the family over for a barbecue. A couple of hours later the phone rang and it was Jimmy.

"Harry, how goes it? You should have said you were building a barbecue, I would have helped you."

"I know you would have, but I wanted to do it myself, you know my first project as a home owner. Would you like to come over tomorrow, around six? I can do steaks and hot dogs for the kids....I mean Robin. Or she can have steak if she wants."

"That sounds great, but I'd better check with Kathy first." Jimmy had obviously covered the telephone's mouthpiece, but Harry could still hear the conversation at the other end of the line.

"Honey, its Harry he wants to know if we'd like to go over there tomorrow for barbecue. I think it would be good for us to get out."

"Oh. No, you go and take Robin." Kathy's voice was low and weak and sounded like she had just stopped crying.

"Kathy, please. You have to go out sometime and it's so close by, you can come back home if you find you can't handle it." There was a long silence on the line and then Harry heard Kathy say in a monotone,

"Oh all right. But we won't stay long okay?

"Good for you! Did you hear that Harry? We'd love to come. You want us to bring anything?" Jimmy actually sounded excited.

"Well you might want to bring something for Robin to drink, unless of course you don't mind if she has beer."

"We'll bring some Koolade. Kathy probably wouldn't approve of a six year old taking to the bottle so early in life."

The following evening Jimmy, Kathy and Robin knocked on Harry's front door and instantly Harry opened it and welcomed them in.

"It's much colder outside than I thought it would be, so we'll eat in the house instead of on the patio. Is that okay with everyone? I already have the steaks cooking." They all shuffled through the house and out into the back yard to view Harry's handiwork.

Surprising everyone Kathy said, "That looks great Harry. Maybe you should help Jim build one."

" I'd be glad to, anytime. I feel like an old pro now." Harry turned the steaks and they went back inside and chatted about anything and everything, except not about Nicholas. Of course his name was on the tip of everyone's tongue but they all managed not to talk about him. Kathy stoically put on a brave face. Harry was putting the last touches to the meal and was expertly tossing a green salad and mixing up salad dressing. Jimmy said,

"I'll go check those steaks for you Harry. Is this the platter you want them on?"

"That would be very helpful Jimmy."

Harry smiled as he said it, glad to see his old friend acting like his old self. Jimmy picked up a large platter from the counter and armed with a big serving fork he went outside to retrieve the steaks. Once he looked at the steaks he thought they could do with an extra couple of minutes so poked them a bit and waited. He heard the back door to the neighbor's house open and waved to Alice as she came out to put sacks of garbage in her garbage can. Jimmy still thought that Harry was dating her and she was on her way to his barbecue and so he said,

"Just in time for barbecue, come on over Alice." Alice realized that Jimmy was obviously clueless about the break-up and thought this was a fine opportunity to embarrass the hell out of that swine. So she stepped over the short hedge and asked if there was anything she could do to help Jimmy. Jimmy had her hold the plate while he forked the steaks onto it and then they both went through the back door into the house.

"Look who's here." Jimmy called as he pushed Alice through the door ahead of him. Harry looked up and to his credit he hid his surprise valiantly. Jimmy instantly interpreted his friend's slowly reddening face as a sign that he was none too thrilled to see the lady in question. He didn't want to make an uncomfortable scene so he pretended everything was as it should be and he would try and maneuver Harry into another room so he could find out what was going on. Alice smiled a wicked smile and went over to Kathy and said,

"So nice to finally meet you, I'm Alice, Harry's next door neighbor." Kathy stood and assumed that Harry had mentioned her to Alice, so she thought Alice knew her name. That was until Alice said,

"And your name is?" Kathy was a bit confused about what was happening but she managed to stammer,

"Kathy, and this is my daughter Robin watching too much t.v. as usual." She motioned Robin away from in front of the television where she was watching cartoons.

"Well isn't this cozy, Harry and his friends enjoying a barbecue. You did say we were friends, right Harry?" Alice facetiously remarked. Harry faked good neighborliness and said,

"Of course. Why don't we all sit at the table and eat. There's enough for all. Salad, baked beans and pickles for any one who wants them. They all sat but the conversation was awkward and sparse. They ate the steaks and every now and again Alice would look at each of them and say, "Isn't this just the best barbecue you ever went to."

Halfway through the meal Harry stood and said,

"I think I'd better check the barbecue and make sure all the coals are out. Don't want any accidental fires.

"I'll come with you. You want me to get a jug of water to douse them?" Jimmy asked.

"Sure that's probably a good idea."
Out on the patio Jimmy said,

"What the hell's going on?"

"We're not seeing each other any more. I can't stand to be around her. I guess I should have let you know, but you have enough on you're plate right now and anyway it's not like there were any feelings between us." Jimmy nodded and then said,

"Watch out Harry, I think she's acting like a woman scorned." Harry laughed at the old fashioned adage. '

"Yeah, right! Let's get back inside before she talks Kathy's ears off."

And indeed she had been talking Kathy's ears off. She had taken the opportunity to suggest to Kathy that maybe Harry had something to do with the child's disappearance. She faked consoling Kathy when she discovered that Nicholas was Kathy's son. The scene that hit Jimmy and Harry in the eyes when they entered the house again was of Kathy sobbing her heart out and being hugged by a teary eyed Robin. '

"What in God's name is happening in here?" yelled Jimmy.

"She said Uncle Harry did something to Nicholas and killed him and buried him somewhere so no one will find him again." Robin wailed and sniffed as she gazed up at Jimmy and she clung to her mother."

Harry blanched and with an incredulous look on his face he turned to Alice, balled his hand into a fist and decked her. It was the first and only time in his life he struck a woman.

12.

Detective Brown was preparing to go out and check on the disappearance of two brothers. They lived on a farm near Woodinville, just north of Seattle and hadn't been seen by any of their rural neighbors for over a week. The local police from that precinct had checked around for the men but had not turned up any clues as to their whereabouts. Their house had not yielded any clues either. It didn't seem to be a case of foul play. Roger looked over the information on the brothers. They were in their sixties, and had lived on the farm since they were children. They had inherited the house when their parents died, and made a living truck farming.

"All ready boss, I have all the paper work, search warrants and field kits." Angela's voice was perky and excited as usual. "Did you see in the morning reports that Harry Prentice, from that house that the kid and those other three people vanished from, was arrested? Apparently it was for assault. He knocked out his next door neighbor, who was at his house, while they were having a barbecue."

"That doesn't surprise me in the least. Everywhere you go someone or other is beating up someone else. Does it have anything to do with our investigations?

"I guess not. It's just that the neighbor was a woman. And you said he seemed so nice."

"Well now that does surprise me, he didn't act like the rough sort. But he was in the army for years and then drove truck in Iraq. Is he down in the tank do you know?"

"I don't know, but I can check if you want me to?" She smiled at Roger and happily turned on her heel to find out about Harry. She was back in a couple of minutes and told Roger that Harry had posted bail and had gone back home.

"If it's not too late when we get back from looking into the brothers' case I think we should stop by there and see what's up with Mr. Prentice. Really I know it's not our department, but I'm curious." Angela always agreed with everything Roger said.

Dressed in a smart short red jacket, tight jeans and stylish red high heeled boots, Angela turned up her nose when she stepped out of the car Roger had driven to the farm. The weather was cold and a drizzle fell from the sky. Puddles and piles of wet rotting root vegetables greeted them in front of the run-down wooden farm house. The air smelled of decaying vegetation, and in spite of the cold, swarms of mosquitoes performed their jerky dances in the air surrounding the farm. Roger and Angela swatted them away as they made for the front door of the house.

"I can't imagine wanting to live on a farm." Angela said with her hand covering her nose and mouth to block out the smell. "It's disgusting."

"It's not if the farm is well tended and clean! I used to visit my grandparent's farm when I was a kid and it didn't look like this, or smell bad because they took care of it." Roger told Angela as he pushed open the front door. It wasn't locked, perhaps because from the look of the place on the outside no-one would figure there was anything worth taking from the inside. It was with some surprise when Angela and Roger crossed the threshold they saw that the living room was relatively clean and tidy. The furniture was old and had seen better days but it was presentable. The kitchen was large and had a big wooden table with six chairs around it, a big sink with dishes washed and drained on the adjoining counter. The cupboards were well stocked with canned goods, and the refrigerator had cartons of milk that were turning sour. Some leftovers, covered with seran wrap, had gone bad. Next to the fridge was a medium sized chest style freezer. Roger lifted the lid and there was an assortment of deli-meats, some steaks and

73

frozen bread, the usual fare expected to be stored in a freezer. There was nothing ominous, no dead bodies or foul smells. There were three bedrooms and it looked like only two were in use. The master bedroom had furniture but it was all covered with dustsheets and looked to have been that way for some years. A thick layer of dust was on everything. After poking around in the rooms and finding nothing suspicious Roger shook his head and said,

"I really don't like these cases when there is no hint of what happened. Read me the brothers' profiles again will you Angela."

"Okey dokey, it says here," she fumbled the paperwork out of an enormous purse, "number one brother, Jake Smith aged sixty-three, single, never married, ex-marine popular down at the local tavern. Brother number two, Jonas Smith aged sixty-six twice married, twice divorced, no children and he's always been a farmer and, like his brother, he is well liked by the community. It looks like no-one would have a reason to hurt either one of them Neither one has been seen since that last really bad wind storm we had a while back."

"Well nothing says they have been hurt yet. I noticed that there was a basement door next to the door that goes out back. Maybe they fell down the stairs and the local police missed looking in there. We need to check that out." They went toward the rear of the house and Roger twisted the door knob to the basement. It was locked.

"Mmm, I wonder why they would lock this door when the front door was left unlocked. Can you see any key hooks?" Roger said as he ran his hand over the top of the door jamb. "Never mind, it looks like there's a key up here." he said as his fingers touched one. He put it in the lock but it wouldn't go all the way into the keyhole. "It feels like there is a key in the hole on the other side of the door."

"The mystery deepens. The plot thickens. The basement holds the dread secrets of the universe. The un-holy are about to pour out of the basement door and into the land of the living. That is, if Roger can figure a way to open it!" In spite of the fact that the missing brothers was serious business, Roger burst out laughing.

"Angela I noticed a couple of screw drivers on the end of a counter in the kitchen, run out there and bring them for me would you?" She was back within seconds and said,

"Here you go master."

"You know Angela you can overdo it with the comedy. Did you ever think that you watch too many scary movies?" He had slipped a piece of paper under the door and was poking the key hole with the screw driver, just like in old detective stories, the key fell out of the lock and he was able to gently pull it to their side of the door. The keys matched so he inserted one of, turned it and opened the door. Stairs led down into a large basement.

There was a light switch on the inside wall next to the door, so Roger flipped it to on, and they proceeded down. The basement had cobwebs and dark corners but not anything special as basements go. It was lined with shelves that held jars of canned preserves, fruits, jams and vegetables. They must have been there for years. Some shelves held an array of old fashioned tools, some had half empty cans of paint, some held broken toasters, and kitchen gadgets, all had undisturbed layers of dust. Roger spun around looking at the room with a practiced eye. No hints or clues immediately revealed themselves to him but when he was about to make his way back up the stairs, he noticed that the dust next to one of the shelves holding the canned goods was disturbed, as if someone had been standing and checking over the contents. It looked as if someone had swept all the jars aside and then put them back in place. There were fingerprints smudging the dust on a few of the jars and on the shelf. Roger rubbed his chin, dismissed the idea of anything being unusual because it looked like whoever had disturbed the jars had decided not to open them. Probably a wise move as there was no telling how long they had been sitting there. There were half a dozen black plastic garbage bags full of litter leaning next to the wall at the bottom of the stairs, Roger noted as he pulled one open and looked inside. Also there were a couple of long handled whisk brooms and large dustpans resting next to them. Roger thought he heard a scrabbling sound coming from behind the shelves, but Angela couldn't hear anything when he asked her. It was probably mice or maybe, this far out in the country, it could be rats. Roger didn't want to try moving the shelves as they were large and heavy looking and he certainly didn't want to bend down and come face to face with a big old rat.

The drive back to Seattle was miserable. The drizzle had turned to a downpour, the roads were congested and the car heater sucked in the gasoline fumes from the cars ahead of them. The windshield wipers did an inadequate job of clearing the rain from the front window diminishing their view of the road. As they sat in the stop and go traffic Roger's cell rang and when he answered it he talked to his superior officer who suggested that he stop at Alice's, the woman who lived next to Harry Prentice. She had called in to say she thought she had an idea of what Harry had done with that missing child. She said she would have gone to the precinct office in person but her jaw was swollen and she had a loose tooth, all caused by Harry Prentice. She hinted he was probably capable of anything. Roger's boss told him to take most of what she said with a grain of salt. She was probably in some pain and wanted to get back at the Prentice guy. But after answering several calls that she had made to him that day, he said he almost felt sorry for Prentice rather than her. Roger said he and Angela would stop at her place and then report back to the office.

Roger stood on Alice's doorstep with Angela by his side. It was cold enough to make them shiver and the heat that poured out of the door, when Alice opened it, felt very nice. She looked pretty bad with a swollen jaw and she hadn't bothered to dress and wore a ratty old chenille bath robe. It was pretty threadbare from a hundred or so washes, she needed a new one. Alice stepped aside to let them in after Roger said who they were and showed her their badges.

"You indicated that you might have some information as to the whereabouts of the little boy who went missing from Mr. Prentices' house." Roger said as he and Angela stood in Alice's kitchen. They had been offered coffee which they welcomed after such a long and cold day. As they sipped their drinks Alice said,

"I'm pretty sure that bastard did the little guy in, and then buried him under the barbecue that he built in his back yard." Roger hadn't expected such a damaging statement.

"Those are pretty serious charges. Do you have any evidence to back up this accusation? Are you sure you want to make a statement saying Mr. Prentice is a murderer?"

"You bet your ass I do, after what he did to me!" Alice in retribution mode looked ugly. Angela was enjoying listening to this exchange as she took rapid notes for Roger.

"Can you be more specific about why you think Mr. Prentice was involved somehow in the kids' disappearance?"

"For one thing when we first met he was totally secretive about the whole thing. When I asked him about what he thought about the disappearance he would just clam up and not talk about it. Then after the police stopped going to his house he built that barbecue. He dug an enormous pit for it, and I bet that's where he buried the boy, under the cement he poured. He would go out at all times of the evening to check to see of it had set. That seemed very strange to me." Alice sniffed and gently rubbed her swollen jaw .

"So you were watching him? Did you see him take a body out there and put it in the pit?"

"Well no, I mean yes, I was watching him, I didn't trust him. I went out with him a few times and he acted very cagey about the whole thing and wouldn't talk about it. That says to me that he was hiding something. Wouldn't anyone think that if they were me?"

"These statements are very serious and the best thing for you to do is to go to the station and make a formal statement and sign it. Then we can get a search warrant and go have a look and see if there is anything there." Roger had the feeling she would back down and not make an official statement.

"I'll do just that, and what's more I think he wanted to kill me last night, to shut me up you know."

"Well that's not really my department Ma'am. I'll let them know that they can expect you to go in and make a statement." Roger nodded toward Angela that they were leaving.

"Do you believe her?" Angela asked as they stooped to get into the car outside.

"It's hard to say. But I do think there is a woman with a chip on her shoulder and some kind of revenge in mind."

"You do know that old saying about a woman scorned and all that, is old fashioned and not true, don't you?" Angela said in an amused voice.

"I'm not so sure about that." Roger said as he turned the key in the ignition.

13.

"Come on Bethany, we can't stare into that thing for ever." Mark said as he put his arms around her and pulled her to a standing position. "Best not leave this lying on the ground one of us might fall in, then what do you think would happen?" Bethany shrugged, she didn't seem as freaked by it as Mark was.

"You say you didn't even feel anything in there when you were swinging the hook back and forth. What if, one of us climbs down to the end of the rope to check if we can see anything?" Bethany looked at Mark and her black eyes sparkled, "I don't mind doing it if you hold the rope still for me."

"Absolutely not!" Mark ran his fingers through his tussled hair and noticed they were shaking. "We have no idea how far down it goes. Are you out of your mind?"

"Well what if we lengthen the rope and get a harness? Then there would be no worries about letting go, or falling." Bethany's idea was a good one.

"Okay, but I'll be the one to go down and if it's safe then you can take a look after I get back up." The thought of actually going down into those depths really frightened Mark. But if that was what Bethany wanted then they would take a look. He picked the frame from off the floor and leaned it against the wall. He didn't want to risk leaving Bethany   alone in the apartment with the frame so he grabbed her hand and said, "Well it's off to the hardware store form ore rope and a harness. Come on."

A couple of hours later they were back in the apartment trying to attach a knotted rope onto the harness they would sit in. They had stopped at the library to get a book on mountaineering and found one with a section on how to tie different knots. It looked easy in the step by step instructions, actually doing it was proving harder than it looked. Mark wanted to be absolutely sure the contraption would hold them safely. It took them a while to do but finally it all came together and was then tied onto the bed frame. The rope had been stiff and hard to work with, but eventually they had a contraption that Mark was satisfied with and Bethany was excited to get started.

'It'll be just like bungee-jumping." Bethany said to Mark as he sat on the edge of the picture frame with his legs dangling into nothingness. The harness, fitted on like a rope diaper, was tight and scratchy through his pants, but the more overwhelming sensation Mark was feeling was fear. He was having second thoughts about going over the edge, and halfheartedly considered offering Bethany the first crack at dropping into the void.

"Well here goes nothing." Mark said as Bethany gave him a big smacking kiss on the mouth. He pushed off over the edge and rather than have Bethany hear him scream he sucked his lips between his teeth and made a humming sound, kept his eyes tightly closed and waited for either a jerk of the rope if he ended up dangling, or a jarring through his feet if he hit solid ground. Bethany watched the huge coil of rope unfurl as it poured into the hole. It was falling in very fast and when it was all used up, the bed it was tied to, began to inch forward toward the frame. Bethany jumped up and tried to stop the sliding bed but she wasn't strong enough. Fortunately the bed was way too big to fall through the frame and it stopped suspended over it, its' feet on either side of it, with the sturdy rope dangling straight down.

"Mark, can you hear me?" Bethany shouted into the dark hole. "Are you alright?"

"Everything seems to be in one piece, I'm not sure about the family jewels though, that was one heck of a jerk."

"Thank God. You sound a very long way away, what can you see?"

"Not a heck of a lot. It's not pitch black but its sort of gray and not icy cold but sort of chilly. That's about it. I can't see how far down it goes. Maybe forever. I'm coming back up okay." Before he started the laborious job of hand over hand pulling himself up, he tried calling to see if anyone would answer him, but no one did. He thought he could hear crying but his nerves were so on edge he reasoned it was probably his imagination. As he reached the top of the hole Bethany was waiting for him and reached for the rope so Mark could catch onto the side of the bed frame and climb out.

"My turn, I'm so excited." Bethany was helping Mark out of the harness and anxious to put it on herself. Her arm touched Mark's hand and she pulled away from him with a little yelp,

"Your hands feel as cold as a corpse. Is it freezing down there? Do you think I should put on a sweat shirt?"

"A sweatshirt wouldn't hurt. To tell the truth I didn't think it was overly cold in there, but now that you mention it I am feeling a bit shivery. I'll put on some coffee that should warm me up. When you go down don't jerk on the rope as that will make it swing around, just yell if you want me to pull you up." They checked the rope around Bethany and she was about to jump feet first when Mark asked about the bed being over the top of the frame.

"You pulled it there just before you stopped, but I'm pretty sure it's too big to fall in. Okay I'm ready. See you in a bit." Mark didn't tell her that he wished she wouldn't go. He knew she was stubborn and if he said anything that would sound as if he were trying to deny her an interesting experience she would be disappointed and probably go anyway. He was seriously thinking of tossing the frame once Bethany came back up. There was just something not right about it. Something otherworldly.

Mark hauled Bethany back up out of the frame when she called out that she was ready and she looked very disappointed as she said,

"We have to get longer ropes, ones that reach to the bottom. " Mark handed her a cup of steaming hot coffee which she took and gulped it down.

"You're right it is kind of cold feeling when you get out. I wonder where it goes to. I didn't see a damn thing but I thought I saw shadows moving out of the corner of my eye, and I could smell something like old dirty sneakers and very faintly and far away it sounded like someone was crying. You said you heard crying right?"

Mark was folding the rope into a coil and was thinking how best to tell Bethany that the frame gave him the creeps and maybe there was a reason why the old lady had tossed it into the dumpster.

"I think we should get rid of it." Mark said as he pushed the bed back to its place across the room.

"I don't. I think we should really try and find out what it's all about. Maybe aliens brought it to earth and it's used to transport things from one place to another. Maybe it's a hole in time that someone discovered and put a frame around it so they would know where it is. Maybe it's a way to move the hole, in time, to different places. Perhaps it's a parallel universe. It has to have a purpose and I want to know what it is!" She looked at him with adoring eyes, blinked her long lashes and said, "Don't you?"

"Well not as much as you do. Come on let's toss it back in a dumpster." Mark implored.

"No way!" Bethany said as she bent to pick up the frame and lean it against the wall. She may have been a bit dizzy from her descent and ascent through the hole, or she may have just lost her balance. Whichever it was, as she bent from the waist she fell head first through the frame. Mark lunged forward to grab her when he saw her falling, but was too late. Bethany was gone.

Mark screamed her name in terror and not knowing what else to do, he quickly put on the rope harness and checked that it was firmly attached to the bed frame and leapt in after her.

"Bethany, Bethany," he called, "Can you hear me? I'm right here, dangling through the hole. If you can hear me shout back, maybe I can reach you." In his desperation to find her he was just saying whatever came out of his mouth. Even if she had answered he didn't know if he had the guts to release the harness and drop down to where-ever she was. The point was moot as she didn't answer him. Mark sat and slowly rotated in a circle clinging to the rope and calling until his voice gave out and his fingers were numb. He came to the conclusion that she couldn't hear him and there was nothing more he could do but pull himself up into his apartment.

The sight of his almost empty room was a stark reminder that everything that had gone into the mysterious hole didn't come out. He was sick with remorse for not having grabbed her before she fell. His stomach was sore and cramping from no food and too much coffee. What could he do? Maybe the fire department or the police could get long ropes and search for her, but if they couldn't find her they might think he killed her, or they would take the frame away and that might totally negate any chance there might be of her coming back to him. He sat on the bed and wept in agony and remorse.

While trying to decide what to do he feverishly combed the apartment for some object that would bring him inspiration. Bethany's cell phone was on the kitchen counter so he picked it up and rubbed his cheek with it. Then it hit him, if he tossed it in the frame maybe it would hit her and she would have a way to talk to him. He tossed it in then waited a minute and grabbed his own and dialed her number. Please, please answer it. It rang and rang but as hard as he hoped that she would answer, she didn't. He didn't give up hope that she might answer the phone, and for good measure he tossed her sweaters in to keep her warm. Then he opened the cupboard doors and tossed in packets of cookies, top ramen and pop-open cans of soup. He hoped she wouldn't get hit by any of these objects. He paced around the apartment, periodically he put his head through the hole and called her name. After an hour or so of doing this he thought he would take a walk to clear his head.

Without a lot of thought as to where he was going he found himself in the ally standing next to the dumpster offering free recycling. Mark looked into it as if he would find a solution to his problems in there. It had a few broken chairs and lamps in it but that was all. He leaned against the dumpster and watched the people passing by. If they lived in this neighborhood maybe they would be familiar with the wild haired lady who had dumped the frame. He started to approach people as they passed and say, "Excuse me do you know of an old woman with wild hair who lives near here?" Most people either shook their heads or side stepped away from him avoiding eye contact. He felt hopeless and went home.

After two days of heart-braking sadness and desperation Mark was coming to the conclusion that it was time to let the authorities know what had happened. He knew they wouldn't believe him and they would question why he had let such a long time pass before going to them. He was trying to put together a sane sounding story for them when there was a sharp knock on the door. Hoping that it would magically be Bethany he jumped up from sitting on the bed and opened it. Of course it wasn't her. It was her business partner Ella. Ella looked like a typical street-fair jewelry vendor. Hers ears had multiple earrings and she had a stone in her pierced nose. Her fingers were adorned with rings and her wrists jangled with bracelets. She looked a lot like Bethany but somehow lacked her sparkle. She hugged Mark after he opened the door and she walked in.

"What happened here?" she asked as she gazed around the sparse apartment, "Don't tell me, Bethany up and left and helped herself to whatever she wanted." Mark's mouth dropped open and he stammered,

"It's not what you think." He was so lost and devastated he didn't elaborate.

"It's alright Mark, I've know Beth long enough to know that this is a pattern for her. It's not the first time and it won't be the last. I guess I should have warned you about her, but I thought this time was different. She's probably moved in with a new guy by now." Mark tried to interrupt, but Ella rattled on and he was too exhausted to forcefully tell Ella that she was completely wrong. "Don't be too broken up by it, if you need a shoulder to cry on, mine is just a phone call away." As she opened the door to let herself out she turned and said 'Ciao.'

Mark couldn't stay in New York, he needed to go home. He packaged up his paintings and art supplies and shipped them to his home in Seattle. He planned to leave the frame behind but as he was shoving his last few belongings into a duffle bag he thought if he didn't take it with him, and there was a chance that Bethany could somehow get out of it, then he should keep it. He wrapped it in an old sheet, then took it to a UPS store and had them bubble wrap it and box it and send it on. Since Ella had indicated that Bethany was unpredictable in her relationships Mark didn't go to the police about her disappearance. He suspected that no one would file a missing persons' report. He also realized that apart from her great personality and her loving him he didn't know very much about her. As he boarded a non-stop flight from New York to Seattle he felt morose and knew nothing would ever be the same again.

14.

When Brian and Mandy, the young married couple, and Maureen had fallen
into the frame they had fallen for what seemed like many minutes and had braced
themselves for a hard landing. Surprisingly they tumbled in a jumble of arms and
legs onto a surface that wasn't too hard. It wasn't wood or cement, and although it
was not too hard, it wasn't like a carpet either. It didn't matter they were so shaken
up it took them a while to catch their breath. They could barely make each other
out in the strange grey light. Brian tried to untangle himself from the two women

but Mandy in her terror wasn't about to let go of him. He was able to separate himself from Maureen.

"Are we all in one piece?" His voice was a tad shaky, but whose' wouldn't be? By then they were all standing and Brian said to Maureen, "How did you manage to get out of here? I can't make out anything. Are there walls? Are there other people in here? Where are we? Is there a door?"

'I don't know' was the answer to all of Brian's questions. Then Maureen seemed to pull herself together and she attempted to explain what had happened to her the last time she fell in.

"First I put my hands out in front of me and started to walk. I couldn't tell if I was going around in circles or not. There seemed to be no choice but to keep going. It felt if I was down here forever and sometimes I would bump into what I thought were other people, but I couldn't see them clearly and they didn't seem to want to answer me when I asked where we were."

"Then there are other people here. If we bump into any let's grab them and make them talk" Mandy's voice was almost a whisper, but a desperate one.

"Sometimes when I was walking I would feel things with my feet. Once I stopped and picked up a can of soup and some crackers. Other times I would hear names being called from a long way away. Sometimes I yelled back but I don't think the callers heard me, so I quit doing it."

"Well Maureen that's a bit helpful, but how did you find your way out?" Brian seemed impatient.

"I just kept walking and walking, eventually I felt what seemed like a wall, so I kept one hand on it, and walked beside it. And I don't mean for a short distance because it seemed never ending. I would slide down with my back leaning against it and sleep sometimes. When I grew really weak I was about to give up when I noticed a dim light, like it was shining through a very dirty window. It was just above my head and I had to jump up and down to see if I could somehow grab the frame and look through it. I did finally manage to haul myself up and I found that the window wasn't solid so I pulled myself over the edge and crashed into my new townhouse, which now seems to be yours."

"Great, now we can form a plan of action because we do know there is a way out." Brian needed to feel like he could somehow control the situation. "We need to stay together and be able to touch at all times and we'll do what Maureen did when she was in here before. Find the wall and follow it to the window."

They began to shuffle along with Mandy clinging to Brian like a Siamese twin and Maureen held onto Brian's belt. Both Brian and Maureen stretched one hand out in front of them but Mandy had no intentions of letting Brian out of her grasp. She was scared that if she did she may lose him and not be able to find him again. No amount of imploring her to relax her hold on him did Brian any good, she simply would not let go. This slowed their progress forwards but since they couldn't see where they were going, she argued logically that it didn't matter if they moved fast or slowly. The absence of decent light and no way to tell how much time was passing made their passage forward an exhausting one and periodically they would stop and rest, sitting on the strange ground. A wall to lean their backs on would have been very welcome. Brian silently prayed they would find it soon.

Occasionally as they shuffled on, things would drop down from above and sometimes they even got hit by things. Usually small, things like clothing, but once or twice they came across piles of kitchen-ware, saucepans and broken cups. They didn't want to be hit by anything that big, they might get hurt. Once they actually passed a young man with a huge bushy beard. He passed close enough for them to be able to almost see him clearly. He was carrying a chair and when Brian tried to get him to talk, he only answered in gibberish. It was obvious he was totally insane and this frightened Brian more than the inability to see things properly. He didn't want to go mad. But in here that might be a blessing, at least the predicament wouldn't matter to him anymore.

A long time after they saw the insane man they still hadn't found the wall, the place just seemed to go on and on. Just as Brian was going to suggest they sit and rest a bit he tripped over something and they all tumbled to the ground. He felt around to see what had caused their fall and to his horror his hand ran over the face of a very small person, it was a child. He jerked his hand away from the face as a piercing scream filled the air. It was a little boy and he had been sleeping. He sat and screamed and eventually the scream changed to intelligent words,

"I want my Mommy. Where is she?" The screams ebbed into sobbing and hiccups. Brian gathered the little boy into his arms and tried to reassure him.

"Its okay, you're safe now. Don't be scared, we'll take care of you, and find your Mom." He thought if only this was true. The boy wasn't very big, how frightening it must have been for him to be all by himself down here. Brian urged Mandy to hold the little boy. He was relieved when she loosened her grip on him. The child's name was Nicholas and he had a sister called Robin. His sister wasn't with him but he knew she was looking for him because she was 'it' in a game of hide-and-seek. Although not the best news, at least it made Brian feel that if someone was looking for the boy they might be found as well.

15.

Harry stood with his legs astride and his thumbs hooked into the belt loops of his jeans. He was watching a police investigation team demolish his new barbecue. First they loosened his beautiful cement job with pick-axes and then used shovels to clear away the debris. He had met some nasty characters in his lifetime, but today he thought Alice the nastiest of them all. He had signed a statement admitting to punching her out, a written apology and promised to pay her medical bill and pay for her lost days of work. Alice was standing in her doorway watching the crew at work. She looked no worse for wear, her swollen face was normal again and she wore a triumphant smirk on it.

Roger and Angela arrived on the scene and Roger said to Harry,

"I'm sorry about this. I'm sure you understand that we had to have this done, if there was even the smallest shred of suspicion we had to follow it up." Harry sounded deflated as he replied,

"You won't find anything. I'd rather slit my own throat than hurt a kid. That's some bitch I live next door to!" The three of them turned and looked in Alice's direction. She stared back at them with her arm crossed under her bosoms as if supporting them. She removed one arm and lifted it to wave at them.

"She's got some nerve." Harry murmured.

After this little exchange took place Angela looked at Harry and was surprised to find that she was rating him from one to ten on a private little scale she used for eligible males. She only did this on ones that she considered worth dating. Harry was aware of her scrutiny of him. He had no such scale, but he knew he liked what he saw in Angela, and had he not been in the middle of this mess he would have asked her out. When it was all over he would follow up on this thought. He gave Angela a winning smile and said,

"It looks like I did a good job on that cement. It'll take them a while to break it up. Would you guys like to come in out of the cold while they work on it? I've got coffee heating." Angela rubbed her hands together to indicate she was cold and Roger replied,

"You two go ahead. I'll just let the sergeant know where we are if they find anything." Harry thought to say 'Fat chance of that' but didn't as he ushered Angela into his kitchen he got a whiff of her hair and thought 'flowers.' Roger joined them a few minutes later and they stood drinking coffee. The silence was as awkward as when Alice had been at his table getting ready to malign him. It wasn't long before there was a tap on the door and one of the workmen asked Roger if he wanted to go out and inspect the sight. They all went, there were no signs of a body. Roger hated to say it in front of Harry but he told the men to extend the digging all around the hole by a foot and to go deeper down another foot. They had to be sure. When this turned up nothing, he told them to fill in the hole. From her back door Alice called,

"Did you guys find anything?" And from his back yard Harry said,

"Can you see blackbirds and pigs flying out of my butt"? With so much tension in the air, the work crew , Harry, Roger and Angela burst out into peals of laughter, a lot of the anxiety floated away into the chilly air.

"You could probably sue her for defamation of character." Roger offered.'

"She's just not worth it and I'm only glad this whole thing is over. My friend and his wife, it's their son who is missing, would probably have to testify in m y defense and I'm not willing to put them through anything like that. It would be too cruel."

D ing, A ngela thought, you just got a score of ten in every category. She smiled happily. Her happy little look didn't pass by Roger's keen sense of observation. H e thought they w ould m ake a great couple even though H arry w as a bit old for her.

A fter they left H arry called Jim m y because he knew that he and K athy w ould have been told about the search for N icholas. Jim m y w as fine and had talked to the detective a few m inutes previously, but poor K athy, who w as w orking so hard to get through this awful time, wasn't feeling so good. H arry offered to go over to their house and thought they could play cards or w atch a m ovie.

It wasn't a good idea so they said goodbye and H arry w ent to w ork on his story. He couldn't concentrate so he went for a long jog. He wasn't out very long before it started to pour w ith rain, so he turned around and w ent back hom e. W hen he got there he realized that the short jog hadn't satisfied. He pulled out the barbecue plans and thought he w ould rebuild it the next day; if it wasn't raining. Som etim es he m issed the heat of the desert and the cam araderie of the other truck drivers. B eing safe from insurgents and surrounded by fellow Americans wasn't all it w as trum ped up to be. It w as just as dangerous here as there, w ith bastards snatching peoples' kids. He wished Nicholas would turn up soon one way or the other. Not knowing what had happened to him was like drinking toxic waste. It didn't kill you right away but eroded you from the inside out.

16.

When Mark returned to Seattle he couldn't move back into his house right away because the renters needed to have a months' notice to find somewhere else to live. He stayed in a cheap motel until his place was vacated. He could easily have afforded to stay in one of the better hotels in Seattle but decided the motel was like a punishment for not saving Bethany. He went to the UPS store and picked up the parcel with the frame in it. When he got back to the motel he took down the pastel print of wild flowers from above the bed, and put the empty frame in its place. He thought that if Bethany were to manage to find a way back out of the frame she wouldn't fall on a hard surface but would land on the motel bed. He didn't paint anything while he was at the motel but paced back and forth in front of the bed like a prowling lion hoping its prey would fall from the sky. Sometimes he paced for hours at a time, like the lion, hoping for a miracle and still Bethany did not tumble out of the frame onto the bed.

While he waited for his house to be vacated Mark went to some of the galleries where his paintings had been exhibited and sold, to see if they would be interested in some of his new works. A new one, called the Gallery Gallactica, had opened in the down town area of Seattle, close to the Pike Place Market, so Mark went and checked it out thinking that with such a central location his artworks would get a lot of exposure. Bill, the owner, was very polite and asked Mark to bring in some of his works the next day so he could ascertain if they would be the type of stuff they would sell. Mark was enthusiastic about showing in a new gallery, as all the other owners had commented to Mark that he 'looked like hell,' but Bill hadn't met him before, so didn't comment on how bad he looked.

After the gallery visits, Mark arrived back at his motel room and saw the cleaning cart was in front of his open door; leaning against it was the empty frame. He quickly grabbed it and entered the room to find the pastel back above the newly made bed and the cleaning lady happily singing as she vacuumed the floor. When she looked up and saw Mark clutching the frame she turned off the vacuum and said in a heavy Spanish accent,

"Senor, you want to keep that dirty old frame?" Mark nodded yes .

" I can get you good deal on new one, my brother can make anything Senor wants." Mark shook his head and took her arm and guided her out of the room . He noticed a pile of 'Do Not Disturb' cards on the cleaning cart and took one and hung it on the door handle pointing at it for the cleaning lady

"You don't want me to clean your room any more?" Mark told her he didn't want anyone in the room again until he vacated it.

"This is my job. If I don't clean this room maybe I'll get fired. You want that Senor?" Mark pulled his wallet out of his back pocket and opened it up and pulled out a fifty dollar bill and handed it to her. She put her hands behind her back and shook her head. After three more fifties she said,

"Senor, no need to worry, no-one will come into this room until after you check out." Mark managed a smile and a nod and a great sigh. He hadn't noticed he was holding his breath. He had come so close to losing the only connection to Bethany he had. He would take better care of the frame in future.

Eventually the renters moved out of Mark's house and he moved back in. Not with a beautiful new wife like he had imagined, but still alone. He was a changed man from the one who had left for Europe. That felt like such a long time ago. He felt incomplete and kept hoping that this was all a nightmare and he would turn around and find Bethany standing there and smiling at him. He needed to let go of that hope and so he figured if she was lost to him he would immortalize her in oils. He abandoned working on his oil landscapes, instead he painted pictures of Bethany. From memory he captured her sometimes naked, sometimes thoughtful and more often than not lighthearted and laughing moments. He painted scenes of her hot and sweaty as she worked on her metal jewelry welding pieces together, or of her in a steamy bathroom taking a shower, and his favorite one of her pinning her hair up with one of his paintbrushes. He hung the pictures of her all over the house and then realized that he would never sell any of them because it would be like selling a piece of himself. Occasionally he would do three or four landscapes and take them to the Gallery Gallactica, as his artistic side needed to be kept alive for the public. Like most artists Mark needed someone to admire his work.

The frame was on the wall in his bedroom and when he first moved back into his house he would stand on his bed and shout into the empty space and call Bethany's name. But as time went by he did this less and less often. He was starting to give up hope of ever seeing her again and his renditions of her were subtly changing. His first versions of her were young and energetic, later ones showed her as more pensive and imperceptibly a little older looking. It was as if Mark was willing her to still be alive and showing what she would look like if she was in his house with him.

About a couple of years after his return to Seattle Mark thought that he would get rid of the frame. Bethany hadn't climbed out of it and seeing it over his bed day in and day out was depressing. He took it down and put his favorite picture of her in its place. He was reminded of the wild eyed woman when he made this decision. She must have lost someone to the frame and waited, as he was doing, for a loved one to come back. Who knew how long she had waited, and when she finally tossed it she obviously blamed the missing person for being gone,, rather than the strange picture frame's ability to swallow people up.

He took it to Bill's gallery as his pictures were selling very well there. He would pretend it was called 'Nothing' and whoever was meant to get it next would buy it and discover its amazing ability. However after he took it to the gallery Bill wouldn't accept it and so he had to take it back. He always took it with him when he was delivering his paintings so when he had seen the new staff member, Maureen, through the large glass window he swept it up with the others and tried to fob it off on her. He felt sort of sheepish about doing this as she had been polite and even joked that he could call it 'Snow.'

A few days later as he started a new picture of Bethany he had twinges of guilt about leaving the frame at the gallery. For one thing, now that he didn't have the frame, his aching longing to see Bethany again was made worse as now he had no physical connection to her. But just as bad was the fact that the frame was dangerous and he had put others at risk by trying to dispose of it. He thought he had better get it back so no one else would go through the agony he was experiencing. He started playing the 'If Only' game. If only he hadn't retrieved the frame from the dumpster. If only Beth hadn't fallen in. If only she would come back. If only he had never seen the damn thing, everything would be really good. He stopped playing the game and went to get the frame back.

17.

Jonas and Jake Smith looked like stereotyped farmers. They always wore white or blue shirts and jeans, held up with suspenders, and sturdy boots. They were a bit on the chubby side and both had thinning grey hair which they kept short. On Friday nights they would shower and shave and put on clean clothes and go to the local tavern for the evening. Jonas, who had been married twice, spruced up in hopes of finding a nice gal who might be a companion for the evening. Jake, who wasn't looking for company, spruced up because it was what you did when you went out for the evening. They were pleasant to talk to and everyone knew everyone else at the tavern. And everyone who met the Smith brothers assumed they were a couple of ordinary farmers who grew potatoes, beets, carrots, cabbages and lettuces. They kept some chickens and on Saturdays they went into Seattle and dropped off their vegetables and eggs to a vendor at the Pike Place Market. They didn't make a whole lot of money doing this but it was enough to keep them in meat and groceries which they didn't produce themselves.

Farming wasn't their main job and it hadn't been their parents' main job. It was something their parents passed to them when they initiated their sons in the job this branch of the Smith family was responsible for. It was either a family curse or a blessing, whichever way the recipients of the job chose to view it as. It was also the reason why Jonas had been married twice and Jake not at all. There was no getting out of this job because the compulsion to do it was carried in their genes. It was as strong as the genes that make birds fly or the genes that cause babies to grow, mature and procreate. When Jonas told his ex-wives that their children would have to inherit this job, both had told him 'not in this life-time.' So he divorced and was childless. Jake saw how this would be a problem for him if he had kids so he never married. The job didn't bother him so he accepted that it would always be his burden. If the Smith brothers didn't have children before they reached their fifties then nature would begin to slow their aging process and a year of their life would be like a second. The brothers were actually quite old.

When the boys had been ten and twelve years old their parents had called them into the kitchen from doing their chores on the farm. It was time for 'the talk.' The boys giggled and pushed each other. They didn't need 'the talk' they knew how babies were made. They had even seen how this was achieved while hiding behind some bushes in a field, spying on a pair of teenaged lovers.

"Do you think they know we know how it's done?" Jake asked his older brother.

"Bet they don't or they wouldn't call us in to tell us."

"Shouldn't we tell them we know?"

"Na, let's see if we can embarrass them with questions. Maybe even ask if they do it." This caused peals of laughter from the boys as they neared the back door to the kitchen. Jake was warming to the subject and said,

"We could even say we don't understand and ask them to repeat how it's done."

"Or we could ask for a demonstration, like the 4H ones we see at the county fair." This was too much for both boys and they were practically choking with laughter and their sides were starting to ache. They went in the house and were greeted by their parents' serious faces.

"You boys might want to compose yourselves, your mother and I have something very important that we need to talk to you about." Jake had to cover his mouth to stifle new eruptions of giggles. Jonas was taking in great gasps of air. He was quite dizzy from laughing so hard. It took them a while but eventually they settled down and then their dad indicated that they seat themselves at the kitchen table.

"Boys we have something to tell you," their mother began, "it's about life and how it works for us."

"You mean how you make babies," Jonas stammered threatening to break out in new peals of laughter. Jake was about to join him again when their father said,

"No boys, it's not about that. We know you boys were hiding in the bushes and spying on a couple of high school kids making out. You were seen and it was brought to our attention. We decided to let it go as that's as good a way as any other to find out about the birds and bees. But if you have any further questions about it feel free to ask." The subject had lost its amusement factor and the boys had no further questions.

"So Dad, what did you want to tell us?" a sobered Jonas asked. Rather than embarrassing his parents he was feeling that way himself. Jake didn't seem as chastised as Jonas felt.

Well boys, we Smiths are the special branch of our family."

"You mean we're all retards?" Jake questioned with his eyes fairly popping out of their sockets.

"I'm not a retard but Jake probably is." Jonas shot back.

"Settle down now. Neither of you are retarded. Perhaps I should have said 'different.'"

Their father looked at their mother as if hoping she would continue for him, She didn't she just smiled at him and nodded as if to say 'It's your job to tell them.' He sighed and remembered how his own father had stumbled over the telling.

"It's like this, boys, your mother and I have a special job, other than farming this place, and now it's time that you begin to learn how to carry out this job." The boys sat up a bit straighter, maybe this would be as good as the birds and bees talk they weren't getting.

"W e Sm iths are also called 'Shtims or Keepers of the Way' and what we do is..." Jake was a very smart boy and he yelled,

"I thought you said we weren't retards! Shtims is backward Smiths."

"One more interruption, young man, and you will find yourself going to bed w ithout supper. Let your father speak for crying out loud." His mother sounded irritated so Jake knew to respond by keeping his m outh shut and not say anything unless asked to speak. Their father continued, w ishing that he w as already done.

"Well basically what we do is to keep a passage-w ay clear of debris and clutter between here and there."

"Where?" From both boys.

"Well, you know we live in this place, on our farm, but this is more than just a farm. It's a conduit to another place. The other place is a place w here som e people get lost in. So w e keep the passage w ay clean and if one of the people at the other end of the passage-w ay m anages to find their w ay to our end of the passage, it is our family's responsibility to feed them , and m ake sure they get hom e safely to where they lived before they were lost." The boys were fairly exploding with questions and as both their m ouths opened to ask them their m other said,

"One at a time , boys. A sk anything you w ant, w e have all the tim e in the w orld to explain this to you . Jonas, since you' re the oldest, you can go first."

"Dad where is this passage? I've never seen it"

"It's in the basement, son, and it stretches for a very long way. We'll all go down and look at it in a little bit."

"My turn! Dad why do we have to clean it, do we get paid for it?" Jake's quick m ind thought this w ould be a great w ay to increase his allow ance.

"I'm afraid we don't get money for doing the cleaning, but we get a sense of pride from a job well done." The boys looked at their dad as if he was crazy .

"I want to know why we have to do it. If we don't want to do it can we give the job to some-one else?"

"Boys it's a heredity thing. The need to do this job is in our blood, it's like eating. After you clean the passage you get a feeling of satisfaction a sense of pride and it just feels right that you did it. You'll understand after you clean it the first time. Our family has been doing this job since time began. It was fist done here by our Indian ancestors and then when Europeans came, naturally a Smith family member was attracted to an Indian one and they continued the job through their children. There are many of these passage-ways all over the world and members of our families take care of them. There are other ways of getting out of the other place. I've heard from family members that if the lost ones can find where they entered they can get out the same way they got in."

"Dad, how do the people get in that place? Is it hell?" Jonas wasn't looking too happy about this aspect of the other place. "Can we go look into the other place of we want to?"

"Most people go in there by accident, or at least that's what the people we've helped out have told us. A couple said they fell in through a hole in the road. Some said there was an empty space in a picture frame and they fell through it, and some have said they just stepped through a door on their way out of their houses and found themselves in the other place. It's not hell like fire and brimstone hell, but I imagine it isn't any fun in there." Jake asked,

"Have you been in there Dad?"

"No boys I haven't been in there and I can't stress enough that you must never, ever try to go in there as you may never come out. You could be lost forever. Smiths are not permitted through to the other side. Never forget that curiosity killed the cat, it's that important for you to understand the danger of breaking the rules. Now let's go take a look shall we?"

As the boys followed their father down the basement steps, with their mother in the rear, they were told the part about the extended life should they not have children by a certain age and that if they did have kids then they would have a normal lifespan. But also they had an obligation to tell the future mothers' of their children about Shtims, as not everyone would want the job for their children.

Their dad stood them in front of the shelves with the canned jams and preserves. He put his hand under the lip of the middle, waist level shelf and had the boys stoop down to see how to work it. He pulled a lever toward him, the whole shelving unit slid forward and to one side, without making so much as a squeak, and before them was a brightly lit corridor. There was enough room for two people to walk side by side comfortably, so the boys followed their parents as they walked forward. The corridor looked as if it was endless and as they moved along there would be small piles of garbage piled up as if blown against the walls. Imperceptibly at first the light started to dim and as they moved forward they could see that in the far distance there was no more light. Not total darkness but grayness. As it started to get difficult to see the trash was much thicker and needed to be picked up. Their father stopped them and pointed to the walls on either side of them, there was a sign that read 'Stop. Go no further. Do not go beyond this point or you may be lost forever. This is the point of no return.

"Jonas, Jake we will keep going over this with you because this something you must never forget. Sometimes when you are down here you will hear people calling out for help, or sometimes they might be crying and sound very frightened. You can call out to them and tell them to come toward your voice and then if they manage to walk out of that darkened area you can help them up to the house. But never, never go toward them, they must come to you, otherwise you will be lost. And it's probably a bad idea to go alone to help someone out, always go together. Do you understand that?" Both wide-eyed boys agreed that they did.

Over the years the boys helped their father clean up the passage, by the time their parents died peacefully when they were in their eighties, they were old hands at the job. They guided four of five people a year to freedom and never once passed the point of no return.

18

The rain continued to pour down for two weeks after Harry's barbecue had been demolished. The backyard had turned into a sea of mud with pieces of broken concrete looking like tiny islands poking out of it. Definitely not cement pouring weather. Jogging wasn't much fun in the rain either so he decided to join a gym, that way he couldn't use the bad weather as an excuse not to exercise. He had just typed 'fitness centers' and his zip code onto his computer search bar when the phone rang.

"'Lo, whose this?"

"Harry, this is Roger Brown, from Missing Persons. How are you doing?"

"Just fine and dandy. What can I do for you?"

"Well Harry it's been several weeks since we installed the surveillance cameras and we have nothing on them. Nada, zilch, nothing out of the ordinary. We thought we'd take them down and give you some privacy. Is it okay if I send a crew over to come and get them? There are a few amusing minutes on the tapes where your next door neighbor is getting 'the, it's not you, it's me' speech. You want a copy of that?" Harry laughed and replied,

"No that's okay. Erase it, it isn't anything I want to be reminded of." Roger agreed it was nothing anyone would really be interested in viewing. "Are you and Angela coming with the crew to get the equipment?"

"No, that's not really necessary and it's another department."

"Oh! You guys don't have any reason to come over here any more?" Roger could hear the disappointment in Harry's voice and he thought he knew what was causing it.

"Not unless you go missing. Maybe I should have Angela stop by with some papers for you to sign, saying that you agree to have the cameras removed. Would that be okay?"

"I'm not fooling you for one moment am I?" Harry's voice had taken on a happier note. "Thanks Roger. She's not dating anyone is she?"

"Not seriously, as far as I know. I'll have her stop by sometime this afternoon."

After the phone call the rain began to ease up, as did Harry's mood. He whistled as he cleaned off the kitchen counters, took two coffee mugs down from the cupboard. He checked the fridge to see if he had milk. He remembered she had asked for some the last time they drank coffee in his kitchen. There was a carton in there but it was almost empty so he went to the local supermarket and bought some fresh milk and also some chocolate chip cookies, who didn't love those? The trip only took about fifteen minutes and then he was back in his house again. There was a crew outside of his house dismantling the surveillance system. After they left he wondered if she would come by in the early afternoon or late afternoon. He thought about calling Roger to see what time she would be there and then thought better of it. You damn fool you're acting like an idiot teenager. Go find yourself a decent gym where you can work out. The morning dragged by and then it was noon, then early afternoon, then late afternoon and then his front doorbell rang.

There she was, her curly hair cut in a fashionably short bob, dressed in a smart blue blouse and matching suede skirt coming just above the knee, covered by a raincoat and wearing a warm smile on her face.

"You got your hair cut." Harry said as he opened the door and stepped to one side to let her enter. "It's very becoming, you look lovely!"

"Why thank you Harry, you look pretty good yourself." They smiled shyly at each other and Harry indicated that he would take her coat. She slipped out of it and they sat at Harry's kitchen table across from each other sipping coffee with a plate of cookies between them.

"Mmm, I love chocolate chip cookies." Angela said.

"I thought you might. Did you have something for me to sign?"

"Not really. Roger was setting us up. He's a really nice guy, and I just love him for doing this." They chatted and the time slipped by and Harry asked if she knew of any good gyms and then as it got later they went out to dinner.

From the house next door, Alice watched them from behind almost closed blinds. She felt the slithering hand of jealousy crawl through her mind as she watched them wrap their arms around each other and walk down the street going toward a shopping center. Men are all alike! Just show them a cute young girl in a short dress and they lose all of their senses. *She'd be sorry when she added a few years and put on a few extra pounds. There were no good men any more and he'd* drop her like a ton of bricks once he was tired of her. Serve her right! A lice reached up into one of her kitchen cabinets and withdrew a box of chocolates. She plopped herself on the couch in front of the t.v. and watched 'Wheel of Fortune' and hated Vanna for still looking cute after all those years of turning letters. I could easily win that stupid game if I was a contestant. Then she had a terrific idea and ran out of the house. She was back in five minutes and sitting in front of the television again, and emptying the box of chocolates.

Harry and Angela hit it off right away. She told a bit about herself and then asked Harry about himself and genuinely seemed interested when he told her about his time in the army and the job driving trucks across the desert. She thought it admirable that he was writing an exposé He thought she was great to be in law enforcement. When they left the restaurant and walked back to his house they snuggled together to drive back the chilly wind and light rain shower.

"Can I interest you in a nightcap?" Harry asked as they stood beside Angela's car.

"I'd love one but it's late and I have to be up early, I'd better be going." She put her key in the car door, got in the driver's seat and rolled the window down so she could still talk to Harry. "That's funny, the car doesn't feel right." She pulled back from Harry who was leaning through the car window and was attempting to give her a goodnight kiss. He pulled his head out of the car and looked at her front wheel.

"Here's the problem, you've got a flat."

"That's impossible these are new tires."

"What can I say? This tire is flat." Harry stepped back into the street and then walked behind the car and all the tires were flat. She got out of the car and said,

"Can you believe this?"

"If it was just one you'd think it was a slow leak, but all four? Someone had to have done it deliberately. I'm so sorry Angela, I'll call someone to come and fix them. Or you could wait until in the morning and stay with me. I have a spare room and I promise I won't pull anything."

"Wouldn't you know it, Roger told me that we were having the cameras taken out today. We could have really caught someone red-handed." Angela sighed and looked tired.

"If you don't mind I think I should just call a cab and go on home."

"It's up to you but I would be glad to either put you up here or drive you home."

"Okay, if you don't mind. I'm really beat. I'd be happy to use your spare room."

Alice once again peeked out of her partially closed blinds and watched Harry and Angela go through Harry's front door. They didn't come back out and after half an hour Alice moved away from the window. "Tramp." She thought.

19.

Mark had his hands resting on Bill's immaculately tidy desk situated in the back of the gallery. His shoulders were hunched forward and his legs apart as he gazed into Bill's face.

"Come on Bill, where's the harm in giving me this woman Maureen's address. She was the last person to have handled my picture 'Nothing'. Even if she did disappear she might have taken it home with her. I'll just stop by there and ask if the new owner has seen anything like it, that's all."

"Well okay, I guess it couldn't hurt to give it to you. But if I do and it's not there are you going to drop this foolishness. I have never understood why you would have put a blank canvass in an old frame and had the guts to even name it. This has to end or I'll have to cancel our agreement to sell your works." Bill's face was rosy with exasperation. What a fuss over nothing!

"I really do need to get it back because….for sentimental reasons." Bill opened a file drawer and looked in personnel files and withdrew Maureen's out from an ex-employee folder. He wrote her address on a post-it-note and handed it to Mark,

"Now remember this is the last time I want to hear anything at all, about anything to do with this picture!" Mark reluctantly nodded and took the proffered piece of paper.

Mark got a map off the internet showing the rout from his house to Maureen's address and drove over to check it out. Once he got there he was very nervous about getting out of his car and ringing the bell. What would he say without sounding like a complete ass? He parked across the road from the house and tried to summon the courage to go do what he thought he must do. He put his hand on the car door handle to open it and saw his hand was shaking. He started his engine and drove around the block again and parked in the same place as before. He did this three more times and as he pulled into the space across from the house, for a fifth time, the front door flew open and Harry came out leaving the door open behind him. He was dressed in sweats, and sprinted across the road and yanked on Mark's door handle and pulled him out of his car.

"What are you, some kind of Sicko? Did you think you would go unnoticed scoping out my house?" Mark started to protest as Harry clung onto his arm. Harry pulled his arm back and had a fist aimed at Mark's chin."

"Whoa, whoa, I'm no Sicko I was just looking for this address. I think the woman who lived here before you, might have had something which belonged to me and I need to get it back." Mark was still furious as he said,

"Are you sure you aren't the creep who let the air out of my friend's tires last night?"

"I don't know what you're talking about! Is this your house now?" Mark nodded tow ard the house across the road. Harry began to calm down. He lowered his fist and straightened Mark's jacket back into place.

"As a matter of fact it is my house. What do you think is in there that might belong to you?"

"Well it's nothing valuable or anything. I'm an artist and I think the woman who used to live here, she disappeared and left all her stuff behind, just might have had an old picture frame that belonged to me. And if it's there I'd very much like to have it back."

The blood drained from Harry's face. He turned quite white, even his fading tan seemed to bleach out. He smacked his forehead with the flat of his hand. Was he an idiot or something? How could he have forgotten the creepy frame? The wedding, and then the tragedy of Nicholas's getting lost, the heart wrenching time before Jimmy and Kathy moved into their own place were not huge enough to have made him forget about the frame? But he had, and Mark, with some relief, recognized that Harry knew something about what he was asking after.

"You'd better come on in, I'm pretty sure I have your frame in my front door closet." Mark became dizzy with relief, and they both went across the street and into Harry's house. Harry closed the door behind them and opened the closet door and withdrew the picture frame that was leaning against the wall. With trembling hands Mark reached for the frame and took it and hugged it close to him.

"I don't know how to thank you. I thought I would never see it again. I have to give you some kind of reward. Name your price I'll pay you anything you want." Harry was astounded at the relief Mark was displaying. He patted him on the shoulder and said,

"I don't need your money, but I'm not letting you out of here without some kind of explanation as to what this is. I do know it has the unusual property of making your hand or foot look as if they have disappeared when you put them in there. You look pretty shaken up, let me make some coffee and you can tell me all about it." Still clutching the frame Mark followed Harry into the kitchen. I seem to be making a lot of coffee for people lately.

Once they were seated at the table and drinking their coffee and after Mark had carefully placed the frame on a highly placed coat hook on Harry's back door, so there was no possibility of an accident. He gave Harry a detailed account of what had happened. He started with how he and Bethany had found the frame in the dumpster. Harry was hesitant to believe that any of the appalling things in the story were true. But it started to seem more acceptable after Mark demonstrated what could happen when he tossed the plate of the remaining cookies into the frame. At first Harry was skeptical. He lifted the frame and peered behind it, he saw nothing but the back of the frame, the cookies were gone. Then he was intrigued and looked around for something that he could throw in there. He tossed in a couple of frilly cushions that he didn't like very much, and slowly began to believe. When Mark told him about using a rope attached to a harness and hanging in there and trying to see what exactly the place was, Harry congratulated him on his inventiveness.

"Oh my God! Oh my God!"

"What? What is it?" Mark looked toward Harry who was standing in front of the frame.

"My friends got married here a little while back and their son Nicholas went missing. We all suspected that someone had kidnapped him when he went out of the front door. The kids were playing hide-and-seek. No one saw him again. He could have gone and hidden in the front closet. The picture frame was leaning against the wall." He clasped his hand over his mouth, snorted a nose-full of air and felt nausea rising in his throat. "He could have fallen through this thing." He pushed his head into it and screamed, "Nicholas can you hear me?" He pulled his head out and said, "He's just a little kid." Mark knew just how Harry felt, and with a quivering voice said,

"What are we going to do?"

20.

Bethany wandered around for hours after she fell through the frame. At first she had just stood up and stayed in one place expecting that Mark would come for her, dangling at the end of a long rope, then save her. But he hadn't come and Bethany began to walk forwards with her hands extended in front of her. One more adventure. I usually like adventures, but I wish someone would turn up the damn lights. *It would be nice to see where I'm going!* Periodically she called out to ask if there was anyone else there. It was a very weird feeling being all alone in this place and Bethany was surprised that she didn't feel all that frightened. To keep any encroaching fears at bay she began to sing. She usually sang in the shower where the surrounding walls gave her voice a nice quality, but in here it sounded like a thin wail, not like her singing voice at all. She had no sense of how much time was passing so she started to count how many times she sang a particular song. At the moment it was 'Benny and the Jets' and the name Benny just kept repeating over and over. *God I hate this song. How many times have I really sung it? After I got to sixty times I stopped counting. I'll sing something else and start a new count. Crap; now I can't think of any other songs, this one's stuck in my head. I'm just about fed up and wish I was anywhere else but here. I wonder if Mark is trying to reach me.*

Bethany kept moving and singing.

"Brian did you hear that?" Mandy stopped her shuffling walk next to Brian with one hand clutching Nicholas's, her other in Brian's, with Maureen bringing up the rear holding onto Brian's shirt tail. Maureen bumped into Brian's back as he stopped walking.

"No, what? I don't hear anything."

"Shush a second. Listen there it is again, someone's wailing or maybe singing." They all strained their ears for the sound. Then they all heard it and Mandy shrieked at the top of her voice, making the others jump in surprise at the loudness of the volume in this eerily quiet place. "Hello. Is there anyone there? Can you hear me, where are you?"

"Maybe it's my Mom, she sings all the time. I know she's looking for me." Nicholas's desperate hope that it was his mother was heart-breaking. No one said anything to encourage him because if it wasn't his mother he would be very disappointed.

Bethany stopped singing and spun in a small circle to see if she could hear where Mandy's voice was coming from, or even see someone. She didn't wait too long to scream back at the invisible stranger as she was feeling lonely and in need of someone to talk to.

"I'm here. Where are you?" She jumped up and down as if this would make her visible.

'We'll keep shouting as loud as we can and you come toward our voices." Brian shouted.

"Okay, I'll try. Don't stop until I get to you."

"I can't shout. My throat's too dry." Maureen croaked. So Brian, Mandy and Nicholas shouted as loud as they could, 'over here,' hoping the newcomer would be able to find her way to them. Eventually a shadowy figure emerged from the twilight and slowly Bethany walked into view.

"Thank God! I thought I was all alone down here. It feels as if I've been walking forever. I'm Bethany. Where is this place?"

"It's not my Mom," Nicholas uttered with his lower lip quivering as new tears began to form.

"This is my wife Mandy," Brian lifted Mandy's hand so there would be no doubt who she was, "And this is Maureen," he turned and stepped from in front of her, "my name's Brian and this here is little Nicholas. We are all lost and are hoping you know the way out."

"Don't you guys know the way out?" Bethany's voice was higher in pitch than when she had introduced herself.

"No we haven't a clue. Maureen's been down here before and so we were thinking she could get us out, but we can't seem to find a wall to follow and find an exit. Have you come across a wall at all?"

"I haven't come across a wall, person, dog, cat or anything at all. I was starting to think I was here all by myself."

"We've seen a couple of people but not very clearly and they actually seemed to have lost their marbles, gone bonkers, gone totally insane...."

"What good news. When I heard you call I thought 'great now I won't go crazy' but now I think I might." Bethany smiled a wonky smile.

Well I thought 'what a relief' when I heard you call. The more of us there are the greater likely-hood some of us will have something helpful to add to the group." Mandy was doing her best to sound upbeat because Nicholas was listening to them and squeezing her hand harder and harder, a sure sign the kid was being scared even more.

"I'm so tired, I have to sit for a bit." Maureen said as she slid to the floor and let go of Brian's shirt. They all joined her and it wasn't long before exhaustion overtook them and they soon all fell into an uneasy sleep.

Brian woke up to feel a breeze brush by his face. Caught up in the breeze were pieces of debris, bits of paper, empty snack food bags, even twigs and things like dried up orange peels and apple cores.

'What the heck is this?' He thought to himself and whispered to Mandy to wake up. She groggily came to and Brian showed her what was being swept up by the breeze.

"We need to follow either where this breeze is coming from or where it's going. It's probably the way out." Brian whispered. He stood up and Mandy put her fingers around the edge of the cuff of his jeans so he couldn't move away from their sleeping companions. Mandy didn't feel well rested after sleeping and thought they should rest some more but Brian was anxious to get moving, so Mandy gently shook the others awake.

Nicholas woke up in a very crabby mood and so did Maureen.

"Just leave me here I don't think I can go on much longer. I feel utterly exhausted." Maureen sounded terrible and when Brian peered at her through the murk she looked as bad as she sounded.

"We're not leaving you behind. I'll help you because this might be the only chance we get to find a way out. If we leave you behind and then try to find you, well I think you know what the odds against that are."

"No really it's okay, I'll just slow you down. I'll just rest a while longer and then when I feel better I'll try to find that wall again." She sounded like she was whining.

"I don't think so." Brian said as he put his arms under hers and hauled her to her feet. She was heavier than she looked. "Put one arm around Mandy's neck and the other around mine. Bethany will you hold Nicholas's hand and hold onto my shirt tail?"

"Sure thing." Bethany said as reached to take the child's hand. Nicholas had other ideas and put both his hands behind his back.

"I want to hold Mandy's hand." So Mandy and Bethany swapped places and Maureen was between Brian and Bethany with Mandy holding Nicholas's hand and Brian's shirt.

Their progress was agonizingly slow as they shuffled forward in a tight group, but the good news was that the breeze was steady and easy to follow as it carried the garbage along with it. Nicholas frequently asked how long was it before they got out of there. No one had an answer for him and after a while he stopped asking, so they moved forward without talking. Maureen got weaker and Bethany and Brian were practically carrying her along. Nicholas wouldn't hear of Bethany and Mandy changing places so eventually they had to stop and rest again.

When Brian thought it was time to get moving once more. Maureen said she just couldn't go on. When they had stopped to rest she had been a dead weight between him and Bethany so reluctantly they all agreed it might be better if they left her behind. Had Maureen not been so insistent about simply having no strength left in her, they would have dragged her along with them, but then that would have lessened all their chances of finding a way out. The wall Maureen had told them about had not materialized so they reasoned that following the breeze was their best bet. Brian was torn about leaving her behind.

"I feel terrible about leaving you here Maureen," Brian hadn't known her for that long but leaving someone behind in this place seemed utterly cruel. "Keep this breeze in sight and when you feel stronger follow it as far as you can. If we get out

I'll come back and follow the breeze in your direction and help you out. Promise you won't wander off in another direction." Maureen was shivering and hugged herself, she nodded her head to show she understood. Bethany saw how badly Maureen looked and pulled her sweatshirt off and helped Maureen put it on. They proceeded on and it wasn't long before Maureen could no longer see them. She sat to one side of the garbage laden stream of air, then she lay down and hoped Brian would come back for her soon, she rested her head in her arm and her eyes fluttered closed as she drifted off to sleep.

21

It was around midnight and there was a storm blowing forty mile an hour gusts around the Smith brothers' farm. It was also pouring with rain and as the wind gusts blew the rain against the windows, it sounded like buckets of water were being tossed onto them. Jonas slept in his room, his snoring was so loud it could have been the cause of the window s rattling rather than the howling wind. He was a very heavy sleeper and since the wind was no match for his loud snoring he was unaware of the noisy storm. Not so his brother Jake, the younger of the brothers, who was a very light sleeper. Jake had heard the wind blowing as it raced toward the farm house before the initial rattling of the windows and the splash of the rain on the panes. He had held his breath in anticipation of the windows crashing in on him as he lay in his bed realizing that sleep would elude him for as long as the storm blew. He got up, pulled a robe over his pajamas, slipped his feet into an old pair of worn, but comfy, slippers, and made his way to the kitchen. As was usual for him when he couldn't sleep he sat at the worn kitchen table with a cup of hot chocolate and a book. Or he would read the sections of Sunday paper that he put aside for later after he had read the main section. There were so many sections in the Sunday paper it took him a couple of days to get through it all. He wasn't sure if he enjoyed sleep or reading the most and if he couldn't do one, then he was perfectly happy to do the other.

As he sat and read, the storm picked up in intensity and the lights flickered a few times and then eventually went out. It was always the same with bad storms, they knocked out the power. Sometimes it took up to a week to be restored. Jake and Jonas often said that they really ought to get a generator, especially during times such as this when the power was out, then the thought was forgotten as soon as the power was restored. Having lived in the same house all his life Jake didn't really need lights to find his way around, he knew where they kept everything and soon the kitchen was bathed in the glow of a kerosene lamp and some candles. The wavering candles made shadows dance on the walls and the words in Jakes book looked like thin black ocean waves flowing across the white pages. He closed the book, marking the page with a thin strip of newspaper that he tore from the margin of one of the unread sections.

It looked like sleep and reading were out of the question so Jake put wood in the stove and lit a cheery fire. He sat with his feet touching the hearth and the crackling fire and extra warmth lulled him as he sat with his hands resting on his ample belly. He was drifting off into an uneasy sleep when, just above the sound of the wailing wind, he thought he detected a higher pitched sound. It wasn't an unfamiliar one, he had heard similar wails many times over the years. It was the wail of one of the lost ones. He knew it was emanating somewhere beyond the passage in the basement so he took one of the kerosene lamps and headed for his bedroom where he dressed warmly. He considered waking Jonas but thought there was no reason for both of them to lose a night's sleep and went down the basement steps alone.

The shelf made a creaking sound as it opened and Jake made a mental note to oil the opening mechanism the next time he came down here. The brothers regularly picked up the litter and so he was close to the end of the corridor before the lantern picked out the dried up food wrappers and pieces of old rags and even a couple of desiccated mouse carcasses. He waded through them until he came to the sign warning not to go any further. The wailing voice had carried down the passage as Jake made his way toward it. He called out and told the voice to answer him if it could hear him. A distraught male voice hysterically screamed out,

"Where are you? I can't see anything. I've been in here forever. Where are you?"

"Try to calm down and don't scream. I'll keep talking and you come toward my voice okay?" Jake's voice was calm, warm and strong sounding, he tried to reassure the lost one. There had been a few times when the brothers felt bad at the sheer terror in the lost peoples' voices as they pleaded for them to come and find them. They felt even worse when they failed to find a way toward the brother's out-reaching hands that were waiting for them and wandered off in the wrong direction and lost the sound of the brother's calls.

"Won't you come and get me? I'm so tired and can't see you." Jake continued to calmly talk and hoped the person would find him. After some minutes the voice said. "I think I see you. Don't go away, wait 'til I get there." Jake set the lamp on the ground after kicking away some of the debris, he didn't want to start a fire in here, opened both his arms toward the man knowing the guy would be very emotional and have a horrific story to tell.

As he fell into Jakes arms he was babbling incoherently and Jake guided him to a sitting position on the ground as he tried to reassure him that he was safe and Jake would lead him to safety. When Jake felt the guy was ready to be led out he helped him to stand.

"Wait!" Now that the man realized that he was going to be saved he continued, "We have to go back for my wife. We can't leave her in there, she was getting so weak I told her to rest and I'd be back for her."

"I'm so sorry but you can't go back there. I'm sure your wife will find her way soon, like you did, and I'll guide her to you." Jake felt awful, as the likelihood of that happening was absolutely, almost totally, zero. The man who looked very weak and emaciated was a lot stronger than he seemed and with an iron grip on Jake's arm he dragged him past the point of no return and said, "I must find her and you can help me." Jake tried to turn and run back to the way he was being dragged from, but only ran into the twilight darkness, the passage had gone. He felt the terror he had frequently encountered in the ones who had been rescued.

The storm blew throughout the night and then just before dawn it moved east. So when Jonas awoke the sun was shining through the last few scudding clouds and glistening on the puddles outside the farm house. He pulled his jeans on over his pajamas, rubbed the stubble on his face and after he tapped on Jake's bedroom door he made his way to the kitchen. He saw a sputtering kerosene lamp on the table and some burned-down candle stubs. He surmised when he flipped the light switch that there had been a storm and the power was off. Poor old Jake always woke when there was a storm and Jonas wondered why, he never even heard them unless they occurred during the day. He added some wood to the dieing embers in the wood stove and put an old fashioned coffee percolator on it to brew. He thought he would let Jake sleep in today as he had probably been up for as long as the wind blew. He could easily take care of the few winter chores that needed to be done by him -self. It was Saturday and he would be taking some root vegetables and cabbages to the market. They only needed to be dug up and washed off. He did that while he waited for the coffee to brew, it would take longer than the electric plug-in they used when the power was on.
    He whistled as he dug up carrots and beets and since the air was chilly he worked quickly. A lot of the potatoes were beginning to rot. He thought they should probably dig the rest and put the good ones in the sheds to dry out. They could do that after he got back from making his delivery. After he hosed off the produce he put it in crates and loaded them onto the back of the old pick-up truck.

The coffee pot was merrily perking away when he went back into the kitchen. He poured a huge cup, liberally laced with sugar and cream. He didn't eat as the brothers always treated themselves to big, gooey donuts at the Pike Place bakery. Sometimes they even ate two. Jonas would take a couple back home for his brother, he would probably be up by the time Jonas returned.

But when Jonas arrived back at the farm house and tossed a bag of donuts onto the kitchen table his call of,

"Jake is your sorry ass up yet?" went unanswered. Jonas also noticed that the kitchen was undisturbed and the same as he had left it. The stove had died and the coffee cold and syrupy. The power was back on and Jonas plugged in a fresh pot and went and knocked on his brother's bedroom door. He pushed it open when there wasn't any answer and he noticed that Jake's robe was tossed on the unmade bed and so obviously Jake was up and about, possibly digging potatoes. Jonas needed a break so he sat at the kitchen table, ate a donut and waited for the coffee to be ready. When it was done he filled two cups and took them outside looking for his brother. He was nowhere in sight and wasn't digging potatoes, and from the look of the patch, hadn't been out there. *Oh well, he'll turn up soon. He'd better hurry though, these donuts are great, I'll just eat one more.*

Jonas whiled away a couple of hours working in a crossword book and then became curious about where his brother was, and why hadn't he left a note if he had gone somewhere. He went through the house and poked his head in his departed parent's room not expecting to see Jake in there. As he closed that door he noticed the basement door was standing open. They always closed it and put the key on the ledge above the door. He went down the stairs and found the entrance to the other place wide open. This had never happened before. The brothers had always heeded their father's warnings about never going into the corridor alone.

They always went together, what could Jake have been thinking? Since it had been a long time since he'd seen his brother a feeling of panic began to descend on Jonas. *Now don't panic yet, wait until you see for yourself what is going on.*

"JAKE, Are you in here?" His loud voice echoed down the corridor and seemed to bounce off the walls. There was no answer so Jonas trotted forward calling as he went. He hoped Jake hadn't tried to rescue some -one and had an accident. It didn't take him too long to get to the warning signs. Jonas felt his heart rise up into his throat. He was sick with worry over finding that his brother was nowhere to be seen and also he suddenly felt very alone. There was no one to get advice from. He could hardly go to the police and report his brother missing. He had no other contact with Shtim s and didn't know how to find them and even if he did they probably wouldn't know what to do as they were most likely also told to never enter the twilight area. His mind raced with thoughts about what to do, and he frequently stopped trying to come up with a solution and screamed for his brother to answer him. He looked down and in the dim light, saw the burnt out kerosene lamp. There was no doubt in his mind now that Jake had gone in there.

Jonas raced back to the basement, up the stairs and out to one of the sheds where he grabbed a wheelbarrow and then proceeded to fill it with all the lengths of ropes he could find. He ran back to the top of the basement steps and tipped the barrow and dumped the ropes down the stairs. After he shoved the wheelbarrow outside, slammed the door closed and raced back down the basement steps he dragged the pile of ropes toward the corridor. He was a bit winded and leaned against the bench to catch his breath. He thought he better not leave the basement door open so he went back up the steps and removed the key from the front side of the door and closed and locked it leaving the key in place. He quickly tied the lengths of rope together and looked around to see what he could secure them to. He settled on the bottom part of the sturdy frame of the swinging shelf.

 Damn I'll need a flashlight. Better go get a couple of them. He raced back up the stairs and easily found them and added a couple of extra batteries to his pockets. He was nervous and afraid, his father's words echoing in his head about never going in there alone, but he was sure he'd be okay tied to the rope and hopefully the flash-lights would penetrate through the gloomy twilight. Jonas tied the rope around his waist, it was very heavy and he plodded forward calling as he went. When he got to the entrance to the other side he hauled the rope toward him coiling it into a huge pile. Once the line was taught he gave it a final yank and heard the echo of the shelf unit slam shut. *Rats I should have checked to see if I could open it from this side! Too late now, me and Jake can always figure something out when we get back.* With a flashlight in each hand he walked into the murky unknown.

22.

　　"Maybe you needed more rope than you used," Harry said to Mark as they both stood and stared at the enigm atic picture fram e.

　　"Maybe I needed help and shouldn't have tried it by myself. I wish I'd called the police, but I didn't want to be hauled off in a straight-jacket." Harry nodded .

"We need to get a team together and figure out how to go about getting to the bottom of this. I don't want to frighten my friend and his wife or even know if there is any hope of finding Nicholas, or your girl-friend. So I think it best not to tell them about this yet. But I do know we can't not do anything at all. Do you have any trusted friends who might be willing to help with this?" Mark shook his head no. He felt a quick, sharp stab of regret at not having made and maintained any permanent friendships. He had been so in love with Bethany that he had thought of her friends and acquaintances as his. But they weren't, and now he wished he'd tried harder to make close friends.

"Don't sweat it. I know some pretty sharp and adventurous guys I met in the army, and a couple of good buddies who drove in the convoys in Iraq. Nothing fazes them. I'll get hold of them and hopefully they'll all turn up with good ideas and solutions. How's that sound to you?"

"Like a life-saver. I can't tell you how grateful I am. You know, for at least listening and giving me some hope." Mark looked like a lost kid himself.

"I can probably contact most of them, get them rounded up, and over here in four or five hours. Then we'll do some brainstorming and find out where the devil this opening goes."

While Harry made the phone calls Mark stood in front of the frame and rubbed his hand over the edge as if rubbing a magic lamp and expecting a genii to appear. One didn't, so he paced around the small house picking up objects, turned them over as if inspecting them and then replaced them from where he had taken them. If asked to identify what he had examined he would not have been able to do so, even seconds after touching them. His mind was on Bethany, she was all he could think of. He put his hands in his pockets and felt his car keys. He interrupted Harry's phone calls and told him he was going to move his car to the front of Harry's house. Harry nodded and Mark went outside.

130

As Mark re-parked his car in front of the house he saw the curtain to Alice's house drop into place. She had been watching him park and Mark thought, 'Harry has a nosey neighbor.' Standing on the sidewalk in the fast approaching evening darkness Mark felt better than he had since returning to Seattle. His feeling of despair was lifting, just a little, but it was a good feeling. He went back in the house and Harry said,

"Good news. I've got four guys who I really trust who will be over in a couple of hours. I had to promise them pizza and beer though. Once they find out what we are up to I know they'll forgo the beer, but we should make a pizza run."

"We should take my car, it's right out front now." They went out and Harry locked his door. As he turned and walked down the short side-walk followed by Mark and approached the car, Alice stood up from the left rear of it. She looked surprised as if caught at something and put her hand in the pocket of her ratty robe. *Doesn't she ever wear anything else?*

"Lost something?" Harry asked.

She became a bit flustered and then said, "Well I was looking for my newspaper, you know that boy who delivers them always seems to miss my step." She walked toward her door and turned and added, "New boy friend Harry?" He ignored the nasty dig and opened the passenger door and got into Mark's car. Mark got it the driver's side and started the engine.

"Where to?" Harry told him where the pizza shop was and after driving about a block the car began to wobble. "Feels like a flat. That's okay I have a spare, I'll pull over here." The men got out of the car and inspected the tires. Both rear tires were hissing and losing air on their way to flatdom .

"I only have one spare I'd better call Triple B and get some help." Mark pulled out his cell and pressed a pre-entered number and spoke to a road assistance company employee. Within half an hour they were back on their way to the pizza place and Harry thought, 'That bitch Alice, she was responsible for Angela's flat tires. What is that woman's problem?' He didn't voice his suspicions to Mark as the poor guy had plenty of problems of his own. But he wouldn't let Alice get away with anything else, she was becoming dangerous. They could have had an accident. The thought of Angela brought a smile to his face and he pulled out his phone and dialed her number. She didn't answer so he left her a message telling her he had been thinking about her.

Mark tilted his head to the right as if to let Harry know he wasn't being nosy and listening.

It was hard not to hear in the confines of the car so he said, "Is it serious?"

Harry replied, "Not yet, but I think it's getting there. She's one terrific gal."

'I envy you,' Mark said sadly, "I was about to ask Bethany to marry me, now I wish I had as soon as I thought about it. Maybe then she wouldn't have fallen through the frame."

"Wishful thinking won't get her back, but action just might. I've kind of got a good feeling about this." Harry's upbeat response buoyed Mark's feeling up another notch.

23.

Without Maureen slowing them down it felt as if Brian, Mandy, Nicholas and Bethany moved forward faster. It was a good feeling following the stream of moving air as it indicated that they weren't moving around in circles. At least they hoped so as they couldn't detect any discernable curves in it. Bethany entertained them by asking riddles and jokes and when Nicholas whined that they were too hard for him she sang nursery rhymes for him. Brian and Mandy joined in, they made quite the little singing trio.

They trudged on until their legs ached and Brian who had the added burden of giving the child a piggy-back ride so they could speed up their pace, suggested they stop again. As they sat on the ground Brian put his hand in the stream of air passing by and wondered where it came from. Did it have a purpose? Was it artificially generated to sweep up the garbage? Where did it come from and should they maybe have followed its source rather than follow where it was going. Had other people found it and followed it. He voiced these questions aloud, both the girls had no answers, but Nicholas did.

"My Mommy read Alice in Wonderland to me and my sister and there was this big rabbit and it had Alice follow him down in his hole and she had adventures and got lost. But Mommy said she was just asleep and when she woke she wasn't lost anymore. We'll probably meet the rabbit soon and then we'll wake up and not be lost." It sounded so logical they didn't know what to say.

"That's probably what will happen, Nicholas. In the mean time I think we should get going again, wouldn't want to miss that old rabbit!" Brian smiled down at the little boy.

****

Not only was Jake filled with terror at the disappearance of the passageway but now he couldn't find the guy who had dragged him in here. It was probably just as well as he began to feel angry about what had just happened, he felt like belting him one. A thought very foreign to Jake, he was a very gentle sort of person. He hoped the place didn't change people. He knew from the stories of some of the rescued people that there were crazies in here. He didn't look forward to meeting any of them. I should have waited for Jonas. I wonder how long it will take him to figure out where I am. Will he be able to find me? Will he even try? Would I, if he was in here? YES I WOULD ! Jake felt better, confident even, that Jonas was on his way to find him. He did what everyone in that place did, stretched his hands out in front of him and felt like a zombie, then proceeded to move in what felt like a forward direction.

****

Jonas's progress was slow, the rope dragging behind him was heavy and he worried about what he would do when it tightened up. He would then have to decide what to do next. He smiled at the thought of the old saying "I've just about come to the end of my rope." That usually meant that the person would give up on what he was doing and adm it defeat. Jonas would never give up, he would find his brother no matter if it took the rest of his life. This wasn't a pleasant thought as he knew that for him and Jake that could be for eternity. He checked his watch to see how long he had been there. It had stopped. Now he had no idea of whether it was a short or long period of time, or even if it was day or night any more. Sweat tickled his brow and he lifted the hand shining the flashlight to brush it away. The beam was then directed above his head and he curiously followed its passage through the murk. For just a moment he thought he saw something dangling from overhead and turned his other light on and pointed that up as well. He must have been mistaken, there was nothing hanging down after all. He stopped walking and took a deep breath and called out to Jake, the reply he looked forward to hearing did not come. He began to whistle and hoped that would be heard, if not by Jake then by someone in here who might have bumped into him. Since he had no way of knowing how long he had been there, Jonas had stopped thinking about anything, his mind was quiet and he kept going, placing one foot in front of the other and directing the light beam ahead and from side to side. The inevitable happened, his batteries began to run down and the light flickered out. At the same moment he was jerked to a stop, he was out of rope. He thought about untying it and going on, but that would be foolish, they would both be lost. After some hesitation, he hated to have to turn back without finding his brother, he refilled the flashlights with new batteries and set them on the ground to point upward like a beacon. Then he undid the rope, gave one long, last call to Jake, turned and followed the rope back to its source. When he got to the shelving unit he tried to find the lever, it was very dark in the corridor and his flash lights were being used as beacons, so he had to feel his way. As his fingers touched the lever and he was about to yank it, so he could get out, he heard voices, a man and a woman' higher one. He froze as he didn't know who it could be or why they were there. Eventually there were no more sounds, after some effort the door swung out into the basement and his mind was furiously planning another rescue attempt.

****

Maureen woke to the sound of a faint bump, bump, bumping. Her eyelids were crusty with sleep and her mouth all dried out from being open while she slept. She struggled to sit up and look for where the sound was coming from. Bouncing along, in the debris filled stream, was a plastic water bottle and it was about a third full. She reached out to get it but a dark shadow loomed over her and snatched it up before her skinny hand was able to grab it.

24.

When Mark and Harry got back to Harry's place, Harry's four buddies were parked in front of his house, so Mark had to drive down the block to park. Since Harry had not told his friends the real reason for the get together and the extended nature of their visit they naturally had talked together, while waiting, and decided it was party time. This was almost confirmed when they saw Mark and Harry, bearing arm loads of pizzas and a case of beer, walking toward them. They offered open arms to hold the food while Harry opened his front door. A lice peeked through barely opened curtains at the group of men going into Harry's house. 'Looks like a party' she thought, 'I like parties.'

"Harry, are you at a party?" Angela's amused voice asked as she talked to Harry returning his 'I'm thinking of you' phone call. The sounds of men's laughter and popping beer-can tabs in the background could be heard. "I'm sorry but if you called to invite me over, I can't make it tonight, have to work late."

"I wish it was a party, and I can't think of anyone I'd rather be at a party with, than you. It's just a few guys I've known for years, we have a problem to solve and this is how we do it, over beer and pizza."

"Problem? Anything serious, maybe I could help?"

"Wish you could, but this is a problem that these guys will probably come up with a solution for."

"Well that sounds intriguing. You're not going to tell me what the problem is, are you?"

"Angela you're a psychic. I will tell you all about it when we are done. Don't work too hard tonight. I, er, um, I'll call you soon." He almost told her he was falling in love with her, but with the guys having quieted down, it wasn't hard to see that they were actually listening to his side of the conversation.

"Well if it does turn into a party I hope you wouldn't consider asking anyone else over, since I can't make tonight."

"The thought would never enter my head. Look I gotta go now, bye." Angela said goodbye and they hung up their respective phones.

Within a few seconds of his hanging up his phone the noise in Harry's house continued until the men, Chuck, Fred, Doug and Will, had all eaten their fill and each taken a beer into Harry's living room and plopped themselves down on the couch and chairs. The four men were all around Harry's age and comfortable with each other. After a few burps one of them asked Harry what the meeting was all about. Harry told them about the disappearances, and about the frame and then about the personally known ones to him and Mark, the child Nicholas and Mark's girlfriend Bethany. The story was greeted with slapped knees and guffaws and 'Good one Harry, been reading fairy tales? Need to lay off the booze.' They changed their minds when Mark brought the frame from off the kitchen hook and lay it down in front of them on the floor. As they sprawled in their seats with amused smiles on their lips sitting around the frame, their expressions did a complete turn-around as Mark and Harry dropped the empty pizza boxes in and they did, literally, disappear.

"Let me see that thing." It was Will, a skinny, wiry man with a swarthy complexion and likeable presence He hooked his toe under one corner of the frame and dragged it toward him, 'I'll be darned, I expected to see the boxes on the floor." He leaned forward and dangled his hand through the empty space. He got up from the chair he was sitting in and leaned over the frame for a better look. Harry and Mark both gasped together and told Will to be careful, they didn't want anyone else falling in. As if willing their fears to come true he pretended to lean even further in, and maybe he had drank too many beers or maybe it was fate, but when he lost his balance and actually did fall in the frame it was enough to make the others believe every word that Mark and Harry had told them. All of them had reached forward to grab hold of Will and all had not been able to, so the problem now took on very serious proportions. Now they all had a personal stake in retrieving the unfortunate people who had fallen in. That was a very sobering thought and each turned to Harry, and he said,

"I know! You all feel the need for some really strong coffee." He went into the kitchen to brew some and found that they had all followed him and sat at the kitchen table with dazed looks on their faces. Harry's three remaining friends quickly sobered up and at first they were too stunned to throw out any suggestions on how to retrieve the missing people out of the 'who knew where'.

"No-go on the harness-chair, huh, Mark?" This was Chuck, a forties something balding man with a little pot-belly and ruddy complexion, asking Mark about his attem pt at rescuing B ethany. 'Did you get any sense of how large the place is?"

'It isn't exactly light in there, you can hardly see your hands if you stretch your arms all the way out in front of you. It feels as if it goes on forever."

"We need some serious lighting in there that's for sure. I think I'm your man for that. You name it and I can get it. We'll light that place up like fireworks on the fourth of July." Doug a big bear of a man, with a tight bushy beard and shining brown eyes, announced to the gathering of m en. Everyone turned to him and nodded. Enthusiasm for the rescue effort was starting to build.

Fred, a serious bespectacled, sm all m an w ith thinning hair and delicate looking hands volunteered, "And what I can do is get the best high-tech robotic survey gear ever invented. W e can send in m iniature drone planes w ith high resolution cam eras and get live picture feed going. It w ill even pick up heat thermal images. If there are live people down there we'll be able to see them. M aybe even see old W ill, silly bastard, w hat w as he thinking, Im iss him already. Can't imagine how you feel Mark, losing your girl friend."

"Thanks, Fred is it?" Fred nodded. "Just having someone else here , and understanding, is sure m aking m e feel a lot better."

"Another thought, has anyone given any thought about involving the authorities, maybe police rescue teams?" asked Chuck.

"For now we thought we'd keep the cops out of it. Mark thought they might think he'd offed Bethany." H arry rubbed his hands together and asked if there w ere any other suggestions.

"Well since Mark didn't have any luck with his ropes doesn't mean that it wasn't a good idea . I've had a lot of experience climbing sheer cliff walls and can get enough stretchable high tensile ropes to reach around half the world. If there's any kind of surface to put your feet on dow n there it w ill be able to reach it, guaranteed." Chuck sounded so sure of this that they all agreed that they now had three good tools to help them reach their goal. Mark thought they should get started that very moment but Harry reasoned that a good night's sleep would stand them all in good stead and they could get an early start the next morning with clear heads and rested bodies.

They all settled down for the rest of the night on couches and in the spare bedroom, and set alarm clocks for six the next morning. Harry and his friends had learned a long time ago how to immediately fall asleep. Soon the house was filled with soft snores except for Mark who would swear, the next morning, that he hadn't slept a wink and had tossed and turned the whole night.

25

Will was the dark shadow hovering behind Maureen. He had instantly sobered up as he began to plunge downward. When he hit the solid surface he had rolled over and positioned himself in a defensive stance, crouching with his hands ready to hit anything that might have come at him. After a minute with nothing threatening he straightened up and looked around. Pushing his sandy hair out of his eyes he gazed around at what was absolutely nothing but an empty twilight place. He felt like a fool, especially since he had not believed that guy Mark's story. He looked upward and cupped his hands around his mouth an yelled,

"Okay Harry, the jokes on me. You can hang a line and pull me up any time now." No one answered and after a few more attempts at calling he quit and started to try and find a way out. That meant just moving forward really, as a person would have to be quite literally standing within inches of an exit in order to get out, it was so dim in there.

He walked for what seemed like a short time when he saw a blurry object. He moved toward it and saw that it was a very skinny woman lying next to something moving. She was dressed in rags and looking like she was about to kick the bucket at any second. She was reaching into a stream of debris that was moving along the ground. It was full of what looked liked small pieces of garbage and as Will moved closer he saw that the woman was trying to grab a bottle with some water in it. Poor thing she looked too frail to snag it so he reached over her and snatched it up. Maureen jerked backwards and looked up at Will.

"That's mine." She croaked and tried to stand and take the water from him.

"No sweat lady, here let me help you." He undid the bottle cap and proffered the bottle toward her. She snatched it from him and gluttonously drank down the contents. He put his hands in his pockets and searched to see if he had anything that she could eat. He didn't find much but there was half a pack of life-savers and some sticks of juicy fruit gum plus a ketchup and mustard packet from a fast-food place. He offered them to her. She grabbed the ketchup and mustard and her shaky hands ripped them open. She squeezed the contents into her mouth, swallowed them down then crunched up the hard candy. She finished this scant meal by quickly chewing the gum then swallowing that down as well.

"Better," her voice was a little less croaky, "thanks. I'm Maureen did you come for me?"

"Kind of, sort of, but I screwed up and fell in here before we had a plan on how to go about a rescue. Have you seen anyone else in here?"

"Yes but they went ahead and said they would try and come back for me if I stayed next to the moving stream of air."

"Was there anyone called, let me think, Bethany or a kid called Nicholas?"

"Yes I was with them for a while." Maureen's voice was starting to sound less lethargic. "There was also a young married couple, they had been living in my house."

Will told Maureen about the planned rescue effort and she told him that it was her second time in there, how she had got out and how she had tumbled back in along with Mandy and Brian. However Will wasn't content to just stand next to the stream and wait, so he decided to try to find a wall to follow. He offered to help Maureen if she wanted to go along with him but she declined, she was just too weak. She was confident that Brian would come and find her and suggested Will wait with her. He was a man of action and couldn't even consider just waiting, he had to get going and find a way out for himself. Maureen said she understood and watched him fade away in the gloom.

A few seconds after Will left, Maureen jumped up and ran in what she thought was the direction that he had taken. She called his name and was surprised at how much the meager meal had revived her. She was luckier than she could have ever known, as Will heard her call and turned and walked toward her voice and then she was suddenly in view and he put an arm around her waist and helped her along. She thanked him and told him she didn't want to spend any more time all by herself in that awful place.

The stream of air carrying the garbage suddenly stopped, dumping it on the ground in a long, low pile. Some distance away from this pile a different current started to flow, picking up garbage and carrying it along just as the other one had done, but in a different direction. This garbage was being funneled toward the Smith brother's entrance and in it were packets of dried noodles and a cell phone. As Will dragged Maureen along they came to the new stream and Will saw the phone and snatched it up and put it in his pocket as the hungry Maureen snatched for the noodles. She fell while trying to get them so Will once more hauled her to her feet. She stuffed the dry crispy noodles in her mouth and wished she could snag another bottle of water as they were hard to swallow. On they went both wishing they were anywhere else but there.

26.

Angela and detective Roger Brown were working late trying to catch up on some missing persons' cases that were unsolved, and would soon be archived in the departments' dead file section. The two cases that had occurred in Harry Prentices' house didn't really need another investigation, so they pulled up the Smith brother's case.

"Maybe they fell down an old abandoned well and couldn't climb out, or perhaps that big storm lifted them up and we'll find them dead, dangling from a tree," speculated Angela as she held her hands out in front of her and inspected her new pink nail polish. On the moon of each nail there was a different appliquéd puppy or kitten that was covered with lacquer. "Or maybe they just got fed up with living on that smelly farm and went to some exotic place for a vacation."

"They would have told someone they were going. They were regulars at the local tavern."

"Want me to check with the local police to see if they turned up and then no one remembered to mention it to us?"

"Sure thing and if they haven't been heard from I think I'd like to take another look around the place. Sign out a car for us. We'll get an early start first thing in the morning."

"Will do." Angela was in a good mood. She planned to call Harry and see if he was interested in going to see a movie.

Sitting next to Roger in the front seat of the car Angela felt bored with the drive up north. She was warmly dressed in a green business suit, wool coat and matching green mid-calf high-heeled boots. The sky was overcast and dreary. The overgrown pines and firs, intermingled with bare leafed maples, looked as if they were about to reach out to the car, grab it and toss it into the darkness of the dense underbrush. The native salal plants and rampantly growing scotch-broom had taken over the sides of free-ways and forests alike. She fiddled with the radio controls until she found a radio station she liked. Roger didn't like it and asked her to change it to something like 'easy listening.' Her response was fake gagging and throat strangling. She turned the radio off and reached into the back seat for her

147

laptop. She opened the brother's file and since they hadn't got to the farm yet there was nothing to add. She typed in the date and closed it.

"Is there something bothering you, Angela?' Roger looked at his assistant with some concern, she wasn't usually so antsy.

'No, not really." She shrugged as if to shake the question off. Roger tilted his head and looked at her sideways. He smiled and added,'

"I'm a good listener. Everything going okay with Harry, or didn't it work out?"

"It's just that he does seem interested but last night I called and invited him out to a movie and he sort of put me off. I guess I was a bit surprised and then when I offered a different day or movie he said he was a bit busy with a project he and some friends were working on."

"Did he tell you what they were doing?"

"No, and when I asked he was very vague. Does it sound as if he doesn't want to see me, to you?"

"Look, Angie, life happens and you haven't known him very long. Just go with the flow and see what develops. There's no hurry is there?"

'I guess not, and I do really like him, he is worth waiting for even if he's a bit busy right now. Thanks Roger, if you ever need advice about your love life just ask." Roger laughed and said,

"I'll bear that in mind, but I'm enjoying the single life right now. Did I ever tell you I've been married a couple of times. Both times not so great, so I have no plans for a third go around."

"Oh Roger, I'm sorry. I do know several great gals who would just eat you up. Let me know if you get lonely." She smiled at him affectionately, relaxed and sat quietly for the rest of the trip.

When they arrived at the farm the sun had broken through the overcast, the place looked a lot cheerier with the sun shining on it. They got out of the car but the smell was just as unpleasant as before so Angela covered her nose and mouth with her hands, her pink nail polish a match for her pink cheeks. Roger pulled his coat tighter around him as the sunshine wasn't strong enough to chase away the chilly breeze.

Since they had no news of the brothers' returning Roger pushed open the front door of the farm house and walked right in, followed by Angela. To their surprise the house was warm and smelled like fresh brewed coffee and a fading aroma of bacon and eggs. Sitting at the kitchen table with a look of surprise on his round face sat Jonas who had stacks of loaves of bread and packets of lunch meats and peanut butter and jelly in front of him. He was making sandwiches and putting them in zip-lock bags. He stood pushing back his chair and said,

"Who are you?" His face was open and friendly, his tone incredulous. "You are the first people to ever walk into my house without knocking. I can tell you right now that I don't own anything worth stealing."

"Please excuse us. We didn't mean to scare you. Mr. Smith, is it?" Roger was as surprised to see the house occupied as Jonas was to have them walk in. Angela's face had turned crimson with embarrassment, she felt terrible for the old farmer. She added,

"We are so sorry. We're detectives investigating your disappearance."

"Well as you can see I haven't gone anywhere, I'm right here!" Jonas spread his arms wide to indicate he occupied a space in the house.

"Mr. Smith is your brother here as well. We did have a report that both of you were missing. Could we just see him for a moment and then we can be on our way, with apologies to you for our mistake." As Roger said this he took in the table full of sandwiches, an open sport bag on the floor containing a whole lot of flashlights and huge stack of lightweight nylon ropes were piled in a large hand pulled wagon, like ones used in garden centers for customers to carry large assortments of plants. "Are you getting ready for a picnic?"

Jonas hesitated and then said, "Mm something like that, yes." He didn't know what else to say.

"Well we should be getting on our way. Is it okay if we talk to your brother for a moment, now. We need to make a formal report that you are both safe and accounted for." Roger felt he owed the farmer a bit of an explanation as to why they were investigating the brothers in the first place, so he added, "When you were first reported missing we came out and investigated. We did go into the basement which was locked from the inside, so we let ourselves in and checked things out, but of course, we didn't find anything."

Jonas replied, "Look I'm sorry, he's gone at the moment and I can't really say when he'll be back, sorry." The detective wasn't happy with the reply so he felt he had no choice but to ask if they could just look around the house and check out the basement, then they would leave. Jonas shrugged and told them to be his guest. He followed them through the house and down the stairs to the basement. He thought, 'good I remembered to close the entry way before coming back upstairs.' Roger looked the room over and nothing different jumped out at him so he and Angela said good-bye and asked Jonas to have his brother give them a call when he finally got back. When he did they could close the case. Jonas said he would.

Several blocks before they were about to pull south onto I.5 Roger pulled the car over to the edge of the road and stopped. He was tapping one of his front teeth with a fingernail.

"What?" Angela asked, "Have you thought of something?"

"I think I noticed something different in the basement. It just wasn't totally obvious when we were in there, but now it's like I noticed it but didn't. There were drag marks leading up to that dusty shelving unit, they stopped right next to it."

"You mean like a dead body being dragged? You think the Smith guy killed his brother?"

"Not like a body, I can't put my finger on it, disturbed dust on the floor and the shelves. We're going back."

"Maybe Jonas has his brother locked up in a secret room and all those sandwiches are for him. Maybe his brother went insane and he didn't want to put him in an asylum, or maybe they had a fight and….."

"God Angela, shush for a moment and let me think." The detective turned the car and slowly drove back toward the farm house. On their way back Angela phoned Harry and he couldn't talk as he was shopping for sound equipment and would talk with her a little later. *Oh isn't he clever, he's building a stereo-system so we can listen to romantic music together. See you knew he was a nice guy.*

27.

Harry's house was a hive of activity with the guys coming and going carrying all kinds of equipment. Alice had stopped peeking from behind her curtains to watch them, now she openly watched their every move through her front window, blinds and curtains drawn all the way open. What on earth could they be up to? She wondered, and maybe if she offered her help she would find out. She wasn't sure that it was a good idea to offer help to Harry, so she waited for him to leave. She was sure the other three or four guys were in the house when he left. Her little plan was conceived earlier that morning when she had gone to a lot of trouble to bake several dozen chocolate chip cookies. Most every man she had ever met loved chocolate chip cookies, but incase one of them didn't she also made snicker-doodles. After casting off the ratty robe, she dressed in a pretty sweat-suit, which was a bit tight, she'd have to cut back on the chocolates, did her

152

hair and makeup and when she saw Harry leave she swooped up the platters of cookies, placing one on top of the other and went next door.

Alice rang the door bell to Harry's but no one answered. Not to be discouraged she banged on the door with her free hand and to her delight it wasn't closed all the way so it swung open. She walked in with what she thought of as her friendly smile plastered on her mouth and when one of the men looked up she said,

"Hi, I'm Alice, from next door." There were tangles of wires snaking across the floors, ropes hanging from hooks screwed into the walls, power cords dangling from the ceiling. On the table were what looked like communication equipment and five or six laptops sitting on chairs and in spaces on the floor.

"I'm Harry's neighbor and I could see you were all so busy so I baked you a little snack." Only Mark suspected that Alice was not a welcome guest in Harry's house so he said nothing as the men stopped what they were doing and gravitated toward the delicious smell of the cookies.

"Go ahead take as many as you like, I can always make more." She proffered the trays and in no time most of them were gone. "My, what is that you're doing? Harry didn't mention he was expecting guests or going to re-model." She smiled sweetly as if she and Harry were intimate friends. When Chuck, who was taking care of the rope and harness gear, went to answer her he noticed an imperceptible shake of the head from Mark.

"Well, little lady no need to fill your head up with what we are doing. But thanks for the cookies." Chuck smiled and put his hand under her elbow and steered her toward the front door. As they got there Harry, his arms full of bags holding electronic listening devices, was arriving back home.

"Alice." He said in a voice that would have frozen salt water, "What are you doing here?"

"I thought the boys could use a little snack. I noticed how busy you all are."

"Well we can take care of our own snacks, thank you. Please don't feel free to come over here again." Chuck thought, 'bad blood between these two.' Alice left, strutting down the short path-way.

"Sorry Buddy, she walked right in, the door must have been open." Chuck hoped for an explanation of what might have happened between them but since none was offered he just took it to mean it was none of his business.

"Things are starting to come together, so why don't we all take a bit of a break. I bought deli-sandwiches and while we eat I thought we could fill each other in on where we're at." Harry sounded excited, he had missed working with other guys and having plans, and carrying them out together. "Chuck, why don't you start, after all you'll be responsible for making sure we don't fall in like Will, and not be able to get back out."

Chuck cleared his throat and his muscular physique inspired confidence that he was strong and well able to hang onto the heaviest of them should they need to be pulled out.

"Well I'm sure all of you have had to clamber over my climbing gear and that stack of 4x4's in the hallway. We're going to make a frame and pulley-system so we can dangle over the frame and be eased down in a harness. We have enough rope to dangle one of us from the top of Mt. Ranier to sea level."

Mark paled thinking that Bethany would surely be dead if it went that far down.

Chuck stuffed the remains of his deli-sandwich and washed it down with a coke and mumbled, "That's about it for me, I'd like to start building the frame after we finish hearing from everyone."

"Doug, you're lights, is there anything you need help with?"

"Not much I can do until Chuck has his frame rigged up. But I'm thinking we might need more power than we can pull from the house supply. I've got a buddy with the biggest em -effing generator truck. Want me to see if he'll let us use if for a while?" He combed crumbs from his beard with his thick fingers. Harry had an amused smile on his handsome face as he watched his friend perform this after-meal, waterless ablution

"Sure that'd be great, Doug. Give him a call and see if you can get it right away." Doug left the kitchen maneuvering his big body carefully so as not to step on any of the equipment piled all over the house. He made his call and then turned back and waved to the gathering with a thumbs-up and said,

"I'm on my way, be back in a couple of hours."

It was Fred's turn and he proudly held up a lightweight drone plane equipped with the latest hi-tech, high-powered camera with remote controlled lenses. He demonstrated the agility of the plane as he made it fly through the house steered by a joystick like ones used in computer games. He pointed to the screen of a small laptop he had placed on the table. The men all exclaimed at how clear and sharp the pictures of the rooms were.

"I can rig two-way microphones on either side of the nose of the drone. What do you think Fred.? Feasible?" Harry asked. Fred thought for a moment, then said,

"I'm thinking not. If they are very light maybe we could put one on each wing. I was going to see if Doug could put high powered lights on either side of the nose, but the extra weight might screw up the plane's maneuverability."

"Well let's do a test with the microphones on, and then when Doug gets back we can see about some lights."

"While you ladies are discussing lights and cameras, I'm your action man and I'm going to start on the pulley. Doug's going to be a busy guy when he gets back, I'll need his muscle to help with some of the construction work." Chuck patted his balding head and made for the living room where he made a lot of noise moving the furniture and piling it up against one wall. He whistled as he worked and wondered about the frame. If we pulled the frame apart would the hole go away, or would it get bigger and bigger. He laid out the 4x4s and nailed them to the floor, making a mighty racket.

Next door Alice was livid. The noises from the banging were penetrating her walls almost making them shake. She considered calling the cops on Harry again. She decided to wait thinking that somehow or other she would get in that house and see for herself what the heck was going on. They couldn't all stay in the house all the time. If she was watchful she knew an opportunity would present itself. She would get in the house and have a look-see when they were all gone.

She pulled a strand of hair across her teeth and chewed on it, maybe that detective, Roger Brown, would like to hear about the noise coming from Harry's house. If she remembered correctly he wasn't too bad looking with his salt and peppered hair and pleasant face. She wondered if he was single. Her hand hovered over the phone but she didn't pick it up because with all the racket going on she wouldn't be able to concentrate on what she would say.

28.

Will's arms were starting to feel heavy from supporting Maureen in spite of the fact that he regularly worked out at keeping fit and strong, so when she suggested they stop for a few minutes he was quite relieved. They sat without talking for a few minutes. Frankly he thought that Harry and company would have come to the rescue by now and little fingers of worry were stroking his brain. Surely this couldn't be real, but his arms attested to the fact that where he was, was quite real. He looked at Maureen through the gloom and saw that her skin was looking translucent, he could almost see her veins. She didn't look very strong and he felt a bit sorry for her.

"Have you tried yelling and calling out to see if there is anyone else close by?" He asked her.

"Well not lately, since you came by. But yes I've called out after the young couple and the little boy left, but no one answered. Then it seemed a bit pointless to do so when no one answered."

"I hear you." Will nodded his head, stood and flexed his aching, skinny arms. He flapped them up and down like a bird and on the downward swing his hand brushed his pants pocket. He felt the cell phone that he had picked up out of the stream of garbage.

"I wonder if this will work in here." He thought out loud. Maureen seemed to perk up a bit and stood and reached for the phone,

"Let me see."

Will wasn't about to give it to her without trying it first. He flipped it open and yelped when he saw that there were bars indicating a small level of power.

"Yes!" he pressed the button for my favorites and there was only one name listed. Mark. Could it possibly be the same Mark who was looking for his girlfriend? He pressed Mark's button and placed the phone next to his ear,

"It's ringing!" He put his arm around Maureen's shoulders and pulled her close so she could hear when someone answered.......but no one did.

"I don't want to run the battery down so I'll try again in a while." Both he and Maureen's shoulders sagged when no one had answered. They continued walking.

Jake felt angry for allowing himself to get into this place and become lost. He should have heeded the warnings on the hallway wall to the entrance. He had called out many times hoping Jonas would answer. Once more he cupped his hands around his mouth and yelled for someone, anyone to answer him. He almost fell down with surprise when someone did.

"Hey, over here." A male voice responded.

"Don't move one inch until I find you!" Jake said. He knew his voice was as desperate sounding as the voices of the people he had rescued.

"Jonas is that you?" But surely Jonas would not be so foolish as to have crossed the barrier into this place; he was a stickler for the rules.

"No, my name's Will and I have a lady with me, Maureen." Jake began to make out a couple of people through the murky gloom and walked toward them.

"I see you, can you see me?" They did and Jake hugged them his relief was so great at finding other people. They exchanged names and Will told Jake about the rescue effort being planned at Harry's house and how he and Maureen had fallen through the frame, but at different times. Jake told them that he was a keeper of one of the exit passageways and how he had been dragged in there by another lost person. He also let them know that time was different here, he wasn't sure how it worked but it passed slower than in the real world.

"I don't know if you wear a watch but mine seems to have stopped." Will checked his own wrist and sure enough the second hand wasn't jerking its way around the watch dial. It was stuck on eleven. Jakes was stuck on one, Maureen wasn't wearing a watch.

"Well great news, I found this cell phone and it works, watch this." Will said as he flipped it open and pressed the speed dial. It rang and the battery indicator bars shrank and still no one answered. He closed it up and the three of them stared at it and hoped maybe it would ring, but it was silent. Will put it back in his pocket and they kept moving hoping to meet up with anyone else who might be in here and know a way out.

29.

The banging that had been going on next door to Alice's house finally quieted down. She sat watching television when the quiet was interrupted, again, by the sound of large truck going by as the engine was turned off. Now what? What on earth are those guys up to? She went to her front door and saw that in front of Harry's house was a very big generator truck that had been parked there. Her level of curiosity went up several notches as she watched that huge bearded man jump out, then reach into the passenger side and retrieve a biggish box. He carefully cradled it in his arms and went to Harry's house. She madly tried to come up with a reason to go next door and be asked into the house. Something would come to her if she thought about it long enough.

Doug pushed the front door with his foot and when it didn't open he shifted the box in his hands and pushed the doorbell. Harry opened it and with a huge grin on his face Doug said,

"Gather round guys, I totally lucked out big time! I think I've come up aces. In this here box is a prototype Mars Rover robot." Everybody laughed good-naturedly gave, 'yeh, sure, you betcha' type disbelieving answers. But when Doug opened the box it did contain the robot, it even bore the NASA logo. Harry slapped him on the back am id whistles and questions from the others about how he got hold of it.

"It has to be returned, by next week. It's going to be exhibited in the Museum of Flight, but we can use it for searching until then. My friend made me swear not to damage it and I adm it it, I lied about what we would do with it, I said it was for a birthday party for some kids."

"Well I sure am happy to have it on loan for a while, and Fred here can probably rig a system of screens to pick up whatever pictures it sends us. A long with the drone plane and lights I'm feeling good about getting a view of something in there." Harry was getting antsy about sending the equipment through the frame, in fact they were all very curious to see if they would get a glimpse of anything.

Mark stuttered about how grateful he was to be getting all this help and was told not one of them would miss this adventure for anything. He replied,

"I'm hoping it's more of a rescue than an adventure, but you guys are great. What's left to do? Can I help anyone?" But no one needed help. Harry had his microphones ready to hook up to the drone and was about to figure out how he could also attach ones to the Rover. Chuck with his face very red from all the exertions necessary for building the sturdy frame to hold the harness, was finished and hadn't needed Doug's muscles to erect it. Fred's cameras were all in working order and his screens for the drone and now the rover were sitting on the table. He taped little tags on the screens for front and rear cameras, so that as he controlled their movements they would have an all around view. Doug was outside the house hooking up cords to the generator, they snaked from the truck to the house.

The watchful Alice just couldn't help it, she opened her front door and walked up to Doug as he bent over his cords checking to see that they were safely plugged in. Then he would be ready to cover them with a tarp should the rain start.

"My but you look busy. What exactly are you guys doing with all the banging and now you've got this big truck. You can't blame a lady for being curious." Doug had not seen her coming and stood up straight in surprise almost bumping into her.

"You'd really have to ask Harry about that, but I suppose you could say we are doing a bit of remodeling." He turned to go back in when Alice put her hand on his arm and asked,

"If you guys need anything, I'm right next door, you only need to ask." Doug thought she seemed nice enough, he'd have to ask Harry why he didn't seem to like her.

Harry, Chuck, Fred and Doug and Mark were standing around the edge of the frame, they had the Rover down into the hole, dangling from a long sturdy rope. It had fit through just fine but they had to tilt it and then straighten it to a horizontal position after it was through. It took a while and a lot of rope but finally they felt it hit solid ground. They cheered and turned on the powerful battery-powered lights and cameras. The monitor screens on the table were picking up nothing other than a grayish fuzzy light. For a half hour or so they had the Rover go in wider and wider circles then finally they got a picture of something.

"Come on Fred," Harry urged, "Can you get it in focus so we can see what it is." Fred worked his controls until at last the object came into focus. It wasn't very big and when it did show up clearly it looked like a battered can with its label, torn, but readable, 'sliced green beans.' The picture wasn't earth shattering but it was encouraging to actually be able to see something. Mark was thrilled and suggested that it may have been him who threw the can through the frame.

"If we can see something as small as a can then we should easily see something as big as a person." Harry said adding, "Maybe now would be a good time to try out the microphones." He spoke into one saying, "Can anyone hear me? Shout out if you can." No one answered. He decided to leave the microphones open so if anyone did speak they could pick up the sounds.

Chuck was very excited to see the can and said he was ready to go down through the frame. He climbed into the harness and sat on the edge of the frame ready to be lowered into the grayness.

30.

As soon as the detective and his assistant had left, Jonas began to pile the sandwiches, sports bags full of flashlights, and ropes onto the wagon and then pulled it toward the basement. It was a bit clumsy but he managed to pull it down the steps without dumping anything out. Once down there he released the hidden switch that made the shelving move aside to reveal the entry way to the other place. He didn't hear the knocking on his front door, or hear Roger and Angela walk down the basement steps behind him. He banged his head on the side of the shelving unit as he spun around to see who was down there with him and asking him,

"Would all that stuff be for your brother Jake?" Detective Brown asked the stunned looking older brother. Jonas looked dazed and gently rubbed the growing bump on the side of his face.

"Yes," he answered, "but it isn't what it looks like."

"It looks like you are holding your brother somewhere, against his will, is that what's going on?"

Jonas sagged and leaned against the shelves and said,

"You aren't going to believe what I'm about to tell you. I don't see any way around not telling you about my brother and myself, but maybe you just might be able to help me. He isn't a prisoner, but this stuff is for him."

Angela, who was standing a little behind her boss, peeked around him for a better look at the old farmer. She was immediately impressed with how honest and upset he appeared to be. Pulling her coat around her tighter, it was chilly in the basement, and turning her collar up so it met her short curls, she said,

"Roger, how about we all go back into the kitchen and discuss what Mr. Smith is up to." Jonas became very agitated and said,

"No, I'm sorry but I have to go now, or I may lose my brother forever. You are welcome to come along with me but I have to go right now I can't waste any time."

There was a frown on Roger's face, he didn't like the urgent quality heard in Jonas's voice. He felt inclined to believe that Jonas wasn't hiding his brother for nefarious reasons. "We'll come along with you and you can tell us all about your brother." It was while he was saying this he realized that he could see a lengthy passage-way behind the shelves that held all the preserves and jams. "I must warn you though, if I suspect that you are pulling a fast one on us I have the authority to arrest you." Jonas nodded as he grabbed the handle on the cart and strode purposely forward, followed by Angela and the detective.

Their progress felt slow to Jonas but to the detective and his assistant they seemed to be rapidly rushing into the unknown. Jonas talked as they walked and told them about the Shtims and how they were born to this task of saving people from the other place. His story was heard with disbelief by the young woman and her boss. To their credit Roger and Angela treated Jonas with respect and said nothing to discredit what he was saying. When they got to the end of the corridor and saw the sign, the story seemed to take on an air of reality. Then when they looked down and saw the length of rope Jonas had told them about, Roger was disconcerted with him -self for not having looked down and taken notice of it while following on Jonas's heels.

"Whoa, wait up Jonas, we're not all going in there before I make a call into the office and let them know where we are."

"Can you hurry it up then, because I feel the longer it takes me to go in there, the less likelihood there is of me finding Jake."

"Gotcha," said Roger as he pressed speed dial and waited for a reply. There wasn't any reply and not even the sound of ringing on the other end of the phone. "Well, since my phone doesn't seem to be sending or getting reception in here, Angela I think you had better go back up to the kitchen and wait for us there." Angela disagreed. This was, after all, the most interesting thing that had happened to her since she had started the job.

"Forget that," she said assertively, but with a respectful smile to both men, "I'm coming along no matter what. How will I ever get any job experience if I sit in kitchens and wait for other people to get things done? I'm probably going to be a great help to you. Did I ever tell I know CPR?"

Roger chuckled and looked toward Jonas, "I guess it's all three of us then. Lead on Jonas we are right behind you."

The three of them were in the murky darkness, following the length of rope to its end and the beacon of flashlights that Jonas had told them would be as far as he had been able to get, the first time he had gone looking for Jake. They felt the unknown envelope them. It was scary, made even more so because, like the other people had experienced, nothing could be seen. It dulled all the senses, all except for the sense of fear, fear of the unknown.

They eventually got to the end of the first rope and Jonas made the detectives jump with surprise as he loudly shouted out to ask if his bother could hear him.

"Maybe a warning before you yell out like that again," suggested Roger.

There were no flashlights beaming up into the grayness, the batteries had died. Jonas had brought a lot of flashlights with him and so gave both Angela and Roger their own. They were the kind that you could wind up and they recharged themselves, but the charge didn't really last that long so every now and then they would stop and furiously wind them up so the light would be as bright as possible. Jonas joined his new ropes to the end of the one already there and they trudged on, hoping to find Jake, or anyone for that matter, before they ran out of rope.

"I think I owe you an apology, Jonas, I have to admit I thought you were giving me a line of bullshit. This is possibly the most unreal place I've ever been to and I have to say I feel kinda lost and a bit frightened by it. What about you Angela? Any thoughts?"

"Thanks a lot boss, now I know you're frightened, I am too. I wish you hadn't said that. I think I'll just feel curious until the rope runs out, and that's when I run back."

They kept moving and periodically Jonas called out to Jake, or sometimes just to anyone who might hear him, but first he let the other two know that he was going to shout. They didn't talk much, it was like walking in a soundless void, so when a very bright light seemed to be making a beeline for them, and was accompanied by what sounded like a very loud, giant mosquito they all instinctively ducked and hit the ground. It zoomed away and was lost in the murk and the sound ceased.

"What the hell was that?" Roger asked no-one in particular. The three of them cringed and when the thing didn't seem to be coming back they shakily stood and strained their eyes to see what had just passed them by.

"It won't take much to convince me that we should all go back." Angela's whispery voice announced. "Maybe there are all kinds of monsters in here. Giant ones, killer ones, who knows which kinds of ones?"

"I don't think so." It was Jonas sounding much braver than even Roger felt, "My brother and I have helped a lot of people out of here and none has ever said anything about monsters. About the worst that happened to any of them, other than being lost, have said they were hit by something falling, like canned goods or furniture, nothing lethal, just small inanimate stuff"

"Well that's good to hear, so what do you suppose that was. Did either of you get a good look at it?" Roger was clearly trying to hold back fear of the unknown.

"I was too busy ducking to see anything clearly. But of course in here, nothing is clear. It did sound a bit like the buzzing of a model airplane. My brother has a couple he flies out in Flaming Geyser Park at the weekends." Angela volunteered. Her voice was sounding steadier and pretty soon she had convinced the two men that it was indeed a model airplane. This was good news, but only if someone was guiding it.

The place was once again silent. They gingerly walked on with their senses seeking the slightest sound or hint that they would come across someone else.

"I think the nastiest thing about this place is that it feels like your next step could be over the edge of a precipice. But if you believed that then you wouldn't take the next step. Maybe people in here don't move at all." Roger mused.

"Thanks for giving me yet another scary visual, I could have gone for the rest of my life without having that inside my head." Angela sounded edgy and not her usually happy self. "I kind of wish Harry was here with us, it seems as if he is on the other side of the world and I might not ever see him again, just when I was getting to like him."

"Angela, cheer up. He's as far away as the kitchen, in the farm house, at the end of this rope. Wait a minute." Roger looked down and didn't immediately see the rope that Jason was reeling out behind them. When it eventually became visible he was relieved, only to notice that the pile in the wagon had dwindled to almost nothing. "What do we do when it's all used up Jonas?" The question was moot. Jonas was swinging the end of the rope in a small circle with a look of sheer sadness on his face.

"I'm not going back without Jake. You guys can turn around and follow the rope back, or," His pleasant face looked as if it might crack and dissolve into tears, "you could come with me. Three pairs of eyes and ears are better than one. I wouldn't blame you if you turned back, it is frightening in here. It's up to you, but I'm going on." Angela and her boss looked at each other. If one or both of them decided to go along with Jonas it would certainly double or triple his chance of being successful. But Roger's mind was quickly analyzing the options and made a sensible decision to send Angela back so she could bring more help.

"Be careful to follow the rope on your way back, and take care not lose sight of it."

It was decided, Roger would go along with Jonas.

31.

Brian and Mandy were whispering together as Bethany and Nicholas lay next to them sleeping. They had decided that when they were tired two adults would stay awake and alert should anyone else stumble upon them and try to hurt them. They had no reason to think that they would be attacked by anything, but the drabness of the place took away all their sense of security and trust in anything. The stream of air carrying the garbage along didn't seem to be offering a way out. It seemed to go on forever with no end in sight. They were wondering if they were doing the right thing following it. Maybe it didn't exit from this place at all.

"Do you think we should turn around and follow it back the way we came?" Brian asked Mandy. "We could pick up Maureen and follow it the other way."

"I don't know what to do. I'm starting to get really fed up with being here. Nicholas whines when he's awake and Bethany acts like this is the best adventure she's ever been on. Did you hear her say she makes metal jewelry?"

"What does that have to do with anything?" Brian sounded edgy. The responsibility he was carrying on his young shoulders was harder because he wasn't used to taking care of people. Mandy could tell he was upset and scared, she was too. She put her arms around him and said,

"Nothing, it has nothing to do with anything." She sighed and then something astounding happened. They heard a whirring sound and coming toward them was a small square motorized robot with bright lights and the sound of 'hello, is there anyone there?' coming from little speakers. It had initials on it and both Mandy and Brian said 'NASA' as the robot came closer and the letters became clearer. They both screamed with delight, waking Nicholas and Bethany.

"It's a Mars Rover. I've seen them on T. V. Oh my God, do you think it's looking for us?" Brian sounded like a relieved, little kid as he waved his arms in front of it.

"I don't want to be on Mars. I want to be where my Mommy can find me." Nicholas wailed.

Bethany said, "It's too small to see us, it can probably only see our legs." She dropped to her knees in front of it and stuck her face in front of the camera. "Can anyone see me? Are we on Mars?" Nicholas bent down beside her and stuck his tongue out at the camera. The tiny microphones spewed static at them, but they couldn't understand if they were being answered or spoken to. Then the original message played over, 'hello, is there anyone there?'

"Look it's turning around and going the other way, we have to follow it. Maybe it will lead us to an exit." Mandy said as she grabbed Nicholas's hand and all four of them began to stumble after the Rover. It didn't move very fast and it wasn't long before they realized it was moving in wider and wider circles and they were behind it and out of the cameras' view.

"Perhaps we should grab hold of it and stop it from moving so it can see us. Then whoever is controlling it will know that it has found us." Brian suggested. He didn't wait for a reply as he threw himself on the little moving robot. It wasn't as sturdy as it looked and with Brian's weight on top of it the small robotic wheels were crushed and no longer able to roll along. The fine line that looked like fishing line attached to it had snapped. As Brian stood, its little antenna drooped and hung loosely. However the light above the camera lens still blinked and the message still repeated, 'hello is anyone there?' Brian sat in front of the lens and lowering his head he screamed at it, "Yes we are here. Four of us, can you hear me?" For a reply they received static and crackling from the miniature microphone. They could have all wept in frustration.

"Oh Brian, you broke it. Now we might never get back home." Mandy sounded like a reproving school ma'am. Nicholas picked up on the panicked sound in Mandy's voice and sat down in front of the damaged robot and rocked back and forth.

Bethany was not so easily discouraged and suggested that maybe they could fix it, but Brian thought they might screw it up even worse since they had no tools and didn't know anything about fixing it anyway. They should just hope that they were being monitored by the microphones. He scratched the young blond fuzz that had sprouted on his face since they had been there, and then sat cross-legged next to Nicholas and stared at the lens.

"We hear you, can you hear us?" Bethany intoned over and over until she got on all their nerves and finally M andy, running her hands through her unkempt, blond hair, said,

"Can it Bethany, that's very irritating." Bethany stopped and silence descended and even the robotic voice stopped repeating its m essage.

32.

Harry's house was fairly shaking with the cheers that had erupted when the camera had picked out blurry images of people. Fred who was in charge of the drone plane and Mars Rover thought the plane had buzzed over someone and then lost them. So he had concentrated on the Rover as it moved at a slower pace, and sure enough they picked up a blurry face and a little kid poking out his tongue, but for some reason the microphones weren't working very well. Harry thought they should pull the Rover out and check it to see what was wrong with the sound system. The exuberance faded as Fred wiped his small hands over his balding head, pushed his glasses with his middle finger and said,

"Guys, I don't seem to have control over the Rover. It's not responding to commands to move back toward our signal. And I can't feel any pull on the fishing line we attached to it. We do have a picture of a face of someone but they are too close to the lens to see them clearly. Harry I think you should try broadcasting and see if we can't get a response from them." Harry nodded and checked his sound equipment.

175

Chuck, who had been on tender-hooks waiting to descend into the place below the frame, took this setback as a cue for him to take some action. His face, even redder than usual from excitement, smiled at his companions and he said,

"My turn, then. I'm ready to go in and save someone's ass."

Doug who had heard the Rover wasn't responding began to feel worried about it, it was, after all, supposed to be returned intact, he hadn't considered that it might get damaged.

"Hold up there Chuck," his voice was sounding worried and his bushy beard quivered as he spoke, "maybe I'd better go down and see if I can't find the Rover first, I'm responsible for it."

"I'll be able to get to it just as easily as you would, and really we need you to be feeding those lights down there. Don't worry I can find it and I'll be careful not to hurt it." Chuck responded.

"Wait up!" Harry said, "The kid! Fred can you go back to his image and clear it up so I can get a better look at him?" Fred turned to his screens and went back to the first pictures of legs and the tongue-poking kid. He expertly cleared up the picture and in minutes there was a recognizable picture of a child. It was clear even with his tongue out, it was Nicholas. Harry who had been holding his breath let it out and a smile wrinkled the skin around his blue eyes and his good looking face visibly relaxed. "That's him. That's little Nicholas. You guys think I should get his parents over here?" The five men looked at each other and then agreed it might be better to wait until they had him out before raising his parent's hopes. They didn't want the rescue attempt to turn into a public circus.

Mark had been very quiet as all this action took place. He was hoping beyond hope that the legs he had seen in the blurry images were Bethany's. Before she had ever met him she had her calf's tattooed with wolves hiding in a field of daisies. If only he could catch site of those tattoos then he would know that miraculously Bethany was alive and well, and rescue was a definite possibility.

"Fred, do you think we could send the plane back in and have it pick up the Rover signal so that we can talk to these people. The microphones are still working, right?"

Fred smacked his forehead and said, "Stupid, stupid, stupid! We're broadcasting but not flipping the switch to receive an answer. We do need to let these folks know that we can hear them."

It was decided to try and get a reply from someone before actually going in. Harry sat at his microphone and repeated his message, 'hello is anyone there?' he added the word 'over' and flipped the mike switch to receive.

Harry had put loud speakers on the walls in his house so he could listen to his favorite music in whichever room he happened to be in. When he had started to set up his sound equipment for this rescue effort he had hooked the microphones into his speakers so when the lost people had heard his message and the word 'over' the men were audibly flooded with static and shrieks of 'yes we are here.'

Their first rational conversation was with Brian who told them he had broken the Rover when he jumped on it to slow it down. This news was greeted with a few groans from Doug but he soon recovered when the men assured him there was nothing they couldn't fix.

The next twenty minutes or so were filled with exchanges between the guys in Harry's house and Bethany, Brian, Mandy and Nicholas. When Mark heard Bethany and actually spoke to her, he fainted from an overwhelming flow of emotions. Harry pulled him off a pile of wires and as he did so he saw Mark's cell phone fall from his pocket and it flipped open showing three missed calls. When he came around Harry told Mark about the missed calls.

"It must have been Bethany trying to call me. I threw her cell in after her, it seems like forever ago, and she must have tried to call me recently because I've checked it everyday since she went missing, and nothing. I only had her number on it. I've kept mine charged but thought hers' probably lost its charge. I'll call her right now. I feel so happy my hands are shaking." He pressed the speed dial, 'talk' appeared in red letters and then nothing happened, she didn't answer

"Well don't worry we will be going in to get her and then you can talk to each other all you want." Harry was feeling very upbeat and it was reflected in his voice. He had just finished saying this when his own phone rang and when he flipped it open he saw that Angela was calling him.

Mark put the cell back in his jeans pocket, one never knew, it was possible she had found it after he threw it through the frame, if the rescue failed this might still be his only link to her.

33.

After Jonas and her boss, carrying flash lights out in front of them, faded into the gloom, dragging the cart behind them, Angela had taken a deep breath and turned to go back to the farmhouse. She wasn't going to leave anything to chance and rather than depend on her eyes to keep the rope in sight she actually picked it up and proceeded to go hand-over-hand, following it to the basement. It was heavy and she broke a couple of her pretty new nails. It seemed to take a very long time to get back to the corridor. It didn't help that her feet were aching as she valiantly marched along in her new green boots. Then there was a faint light ahead and when she reached the entrance she dropped the heavy rope. Walking without it felt like she was floating along the corridor to the basement entrance. As she mounted the basement stairs to the kitchen she felt the muscles tighten in her legs and looked forward to sitting down.

Back in the farm house kitchen Angela saw that the sun had gone down and it was much later than she thought it would be. She slipped her coat off and thought about which agency to call in Seattle. She knew this was an emergency, but the situation sounded preposterous. If she tried to explain what had just happened to her, to anyone at work, they would think it was a prank. It would probably be viewed in the same way if she called the local police station. It definitely felt as if the only person she could talk to about this would be Harry. But what if he thought she was crazy? She bit her lip and pulled out her phone from her suit pocket. As she did so she noticed that her hands were filthy and her suit and coat were grubby from the rope that had rubbed against them. 'I must look terrible,' she thought as she ruffled her curls with a grubby hand and dialed Harry's number. "Please, please answer," she said aloud as the phone on the other end rang and rang.

"Hello, Harry here, please leave a short message and your number, and I'll get back to you as soon as I can." A beep followed and Angela's voice was as close to sounding hysterical as it had ever been. She left a message leaving her number and also the number displayed on the old rotary phone on the kitchen wall. She couldn't sit still and wait for the phone to ring so she found the bathroom and washed her hands and face, dabbed at her soiled suit with a wash cloth, saw that it was hopeless to even attempt to clean it, and went back to the kitchen. She couldn't find any tea bags in the brothers' cupboards so settled on making a pot of coffee. Who knew, maybe Roger and Jonas would come back and need some too. That didn't happen and so after an hour she redialed Harry. This time he picked up the phone.

"Angela, good to hear your voice."

"Harry you're never going to believe what I have to tell you, it's too unreal, I'm not sure that I believe what's happening, but I have to tell you. Promise not to hang up on me. I don't think I could take that right now. You won't hang up will you?" this all came out in one breath and Harry smiled and thought she was so delightful, nothing could be as bad as what was going on in his house at the moment.

"I won't hang up. Calm down and go slowly. I do need you to know that I'm caught up in something right now and I don't want you to feel offended if I have to leave suddenly."

Angela gulped in a deep breath of air and poured out her story about the missing brothers and how they were some sort of guardians to another place that was scary, dark and people went missing there. She had been in this place and followed a rope and was now waiting to see what would happen. She needed Harry to come to where she was because she didn't really think her bosses would believe what she had just told him. And her boss Roger had gone in there to the end of the marking rope with Jonas looking for the younger brother Jake and walked off into the gloom. Roger had asked her to get help but she didn't want to be locked up in the looney-bin for making up stories. "I swear every word I've said is true. Harry?"

Harry was stunned. Was it possible for there to be other ways into this incredible place? What kind of co-incidence would have to happen for both he and Angela to be in parallel predicaments?

"Angela, believe it or not I think I know about this place." Harry hadn't known that he was gripping his phone so tightly that the composite plastic was starting to make cracking sounds. It must have been loud enough to be picked up on Angela's phone.

"What's that cracking sound? Are you still there?"

Harry relaxed his grip and reassured her that he was still there. Then he said,

"Look I need to talk to the guys about this, can I call you back in a few?"

"Yes, but Harry don't take too long it's a bit scary being here all by myself, and it's almost dark outside now and there aren't any houses really close by. I'm not usually such a wimp but this whole idea is creepy and now I wish Roger hadn't gone along with that Jonas guy."

"I'll get back to you as soon as I can. Do you know what the address is where you are?"

Angela gave it to him and they disconnected from each other. Harry went to talk with his friends who were lowering Chuck, who was dangling over the frame in his harness, into the murky depths.

Harry talked to his friends and Mark. He let them know that he needed to go out to where Angela was. He also told them the story she had just told him, and they replied incredulously that maybe the two places were connected. They agreed that as strange as it sounded it was a possibility. Harry made sure they had his phone number and the address where Angela was. He knew his friends well and had every confidence that they would work as hard as anyone at getting Nicholas and the people he was with, out of that place. He called Angela and told her he was on his way and it would take maybe a little more than an hour for him to get there.

From the window next door, Alice watched as Harry got in his car and drove away.

34.

Dressed in her pajamas and ready for her own bed, Kathy tucked her blond hair behind her ear as she bent and kissed Robin as the child slept. Robin's sandy hair was tangled and sticking to her slightly flushed face. The little girl was growing and her schoolbooks were scattered across her bedroom floor. Kathy straightened and surveyed the room. It had a child's lived in feel about it. She gathered the books and put them in a neat pile on Robin's desk come dressing-table, she didn't want her daughter tripping on them should she need to get up during the night. She tip-toed out of Robin's room, hesitated near the door of the room that was meant for Nicholas and silently pushed it open and turned on the light and peeked in. It was exactly the same as it had been when she had first seen how Jimmy and Harry had fixed it up for her little boy. She didn't choke up and turn and flee from the room as she usually did when she went in there. It was not empty but it felt that way without Nicholas sleeping and playing in it, she turned and left the room closing the door behind her.

Jimmy, her husband, was noisily doing push-ups on the bedroom floor. He did one hundred every morning and night telling Kathy he wanted to keep fit. After the push-ups he did one hundred sit-ups. At the start of their marriage Jimmy had invited Kathy to join him in these exercises thinking they might help relieve her

183

stress over her lost son. She had half-heartedly tried a couple of times and then told him exercise wasn't any fun so she would just watch him. He didn't push her and every now and then he offered to go very slowly if she wanted to join him in the exercises. She always declined so it was a bit of a surprise when that evening she said,

"Jimmy I've been thinking. What would you say about turning Nicholas's room into a gym?" Jimmy stopped in mid push-up his face red from exertion and his blue eyes slightly bulging. He jumped up, his tall lean body oozing sweat. He enfolded Kathy with his arms and sweat leached into her pajama top.

"Honey don't you think it's a bit soon to be giving up on the little guy being found?"

Kathy swallowed hard before answering, "Maybe, but passing by that closed door all the time only reminds me that he is gone."

"We could leave it open."

"That wouldn't help, it's full of his things. I think it best if we package them up and maybe send them to the goodwill."

Jimmy nodded his head. Then he shook his head.

"No, we're not giving anything away. Not yet. If it helps to open up the room and put his things away then that's what we'll do. The three of us can do it together and then decide what to use the room for. Anyway I don't really care to have a gym-room in the house. The equipment is expensive and takes up too much space. Besides if nature meant for us to use gym equipment she would have given us built in, well I don't know what, wings?" Kathy smiled at his feeble attempt at levity and loved him for it.

"You know what?" she said, "You smell and now so do I. Race you to the shower." Life for them was starting to flow to a rhythm, and normalcy was seeping into their lives together.

35.

By the time Harry got to the Smith brother's farm it was completely dark and foggy and he hoped he was at the right place. The farm house he pulled up to had every light in the house blazing and all the outdoor lights had yellow halos around them glowing through the fog. He parked next to Roger's official car and had barely turned off the engine to his, when Angela came flying out of the front door. As he stood from getting out of his car she was in his arms and squeezing the breath out of him .

"Harry I thought you'd never get here. I called you several times but you didn't pick up." Harry reached into his pocket, no easy feat as Angela was clinging to him like a grape vine, and noticed that it needed re-charging. When she finally let go of him they walked hand in hand to the farm house and went into the kitchen. The brilliant lights bathed every nook and cranny and not a few dusty cobwebs were showing, they were probably missed in the softer light of day.

"It sounds like you've had quite a day. How about you pour some of that coffee and bring me up to date on what's been happening here." Now that Harry was there and she wasn't all alone in the house she poured out her story of how detective Roger Brown had wanted to close the file on the missing brothers. Then when they had arrived at the farm house the older brother Jonas had been in the kitchen and acting suspiciously, if you could call making mountains of sandwiches

185

suspicious. Then they had left to go back into Seattle and Roger had a hunch that something was wrong, so they went back and Jonas told them his story. At first she had thought he was telling them a trumped up story but she and Roger had certainly believed him after they followed the corridor into the weird place. But they hadn't found the brother Jake, so Angela had made her way back to the farm house alone. Harry quickly brought Angela up to date on what had been going on at his house.

As Harry and Angela sat across from each other gulping coffee, Harry was thinking and then as his thoughts coalesced,

"Angela as soon as we finish our coffee I want to go and look at this entranceway. You say it opens into the place even though you can't see in there for very far?"

"Yes that's right but we had flashlights when we all went in, but to tell the truth they don't help that much. You're planning on trying to rescue Roger and Jonas aren't you?"

"Eventually, yes of course. But you know what I'm thinking now, is that it has to be a lot easier going in there at ground level rather than hanging in from a rope and harness through a picture frame. Wouldn't you say so?"

"Harry you're brilliant," Harry almost blushed at the adoration flowing from Angela's eyes, "you would make a great detective." Harry stood and pulled Angela to her feet and gave her lips a quick kiss and then asked her to lead the way to the basement.

They stopped at the end of the corridor and Harry bent and inspected the rope. Taking Angela's hand they followed it to its end and there was no sign of either Roger or Jonas. They called a few times but no one answered. They returned to the farm house kitchen.

"Yes Mark, what I'm saying is , I think we have a better shot at getting them all out at this end." Harry had called his house and Mark had answered the phone . Harry told him about the entryway at the farm house. Mark was reluctant to abandon the picture frame entry for the uncertain new avenue. Harry asked to speak to either, Chuck, Doug or Fred. He talked to each of them and they all agreed that the farm house was probably the best way to go . Easier to get their equipment into the other place and as long as they brought the generator truck along with them power would not be a problem . So it was decided, in spite of Mark's insistence that he thought since the house had proved to be a conduit to Bethany, Nicholas and the people they were with . His objections were over-ruled by the others and with some trepidation he helped the men gather the sound equipment, lights, computers and monitors and carefully pack them up and get ready to join Harry and Angela. They retrieved the drone plane but the Mars Rover wouldn't respond to any commands. Mark wanted to take the picture frame as well but it was nailed firmly in place and the other guys thought that it best to leave it where it was in case the entry way at the farm house didn't pan out. He helped carry the miles of rope to Chuck's van, but they left the harness dangling above the frame. Chuck hadn't seen or heard anything when he had lowered himself down for what seemed like a long way, so the idea of a corridor seemed like a much better way to go in .

From her house Alice watched them pile into the vehicles and leave.

It was early morning by the time the power truck, van and Mark's car arrived at the farm house. Angela and Harry had spent the time waiting for them , amiably getting to know each other better and sweeping the corridor as there would be yards of power cords and rope to be stretched along its length and further. The packing up and journey to the farm house had left the men drained of energy along with Harry and Angela. They decided to take a three-hour power-nap. Mark couldn't sleep and so he went to the nearest 24/7 market and bought eggs, bacon, cereal and pancake-mix, milk and syrup. If he couldn't sleep he could at least be productive and fix the guys a decent breakfast. Who knew, maybe soon he would be fixing a breakfast for Bethany.

The aroma of bacon and eggs and coffee wafted throughout the house and woke everyone. They all ate as if it might be their last meal. They planned as they ate and slurped coffee and when they were done with the meal they began to set up their equipment. It wasn't long before power cords snaked from the power truck through the house and down the basement steps and along the passage to the entrance to the other place. Chuck attached more rope to the end of the one that Angela had followed back to the house.

"Definitely creepy in there," he announced to everyone when he returned, "but a helluva lot easier to take when you're not dangling from the end of a rope sitting in a harness."

The drone plane was checked out and adjustments made to its lights and microphones and speakers. Angela watched as Harry worked on them then suddenly burst out laughing.

"Here I thought you were buying sound equipment to play romantic music for me. But it was for this wasn't it?" Harry nodded and said,

"Don't worry I'll be happy to play romantic music for you when this is all over." They both looked up to see the guys grinning at them.

"Should we suggest they get a room?" Fred said as he took the plane from Harry. The men all laughed and Angela laughed along with them, blushing and not really minding the friendly teasing. Then serious planning began and Angela realized that having Harry so close was great but she was very worried about her boss, Roger, and to some extent Jonas and his brother Jake.

36.

Roger was starting to feel that going along with Jonas was futile. He didn't know how long they had been slowly moving....forward? Their flashlights barely penetrated the gloom, they hadn't seen a single soul and Jonas was the least communicative person Roger had ever met. He missed Angela's inane chatter, at least with her there were no long and extended silences. Jason could hardly bring himself to give Roger a muttered grunt to any questions asked of him. Roger began to think he should turn back and take a chance at finding the rope-end that led to the exit. For all he knew they were walking in circles. He said as much to Jonas.

"Detective, I'm sorry. I should have told you not to come. I've spent my whole life with my brother. I can't explain the loss to you. It's like losing a Siamese twin. Our bond is very strong, that's why I feel that I can find him. It wasn't right of me to let you come along." Roger was surprised at the reply but at least he felt better about being with the man. Maybe Jonas even knew how to find a way out, but had failed to mention that fact. He asked him and got the deflating reply of 'they would cross that bridge after they found Jake.'

Jake, Will and Maureen were resting. They had finally bumped into a wall. Maureen had been elated. She told them how she had first found a wall and followed it to what she had thought was a window, but it had turned out to be the frame and she had ended up in her own house. Unfortunately she had fallen back in when the curious young couple Brian and Mandy, who were then living in her house, had leaned too far into the frame and dragged her back in with them . They were resting because Maureen told them that it wasn't easy finding the exit, they could follow the wall and not find one. Jake told them that there were several ways to exit the place, not just the place where they had managed to get in. They were quiet for a while when Will said,

"Did anyone hear a scuffling sound?" They each held their breath and strained their ears to pick up any sounds. They peered into the gloom and soon faint lights seemed to be pointing at them and getting closer. "Is that you Harry?" yelled Will as he rose to meet the oncoming lights. Maureen grabbed Will's shirt and whispered,

"Let them come to us, it might not be anyone you'd want to meet."

But although the lights weren't carried by Harry they were carried by Jonas and Detective Roger Brown. The two aging brothers fell into each others arms and unashamedly wept together. Maureen, Will and Roger had silly grins on their faces feeling the relief emanating from the two men, and for just a second they thought that, just maybe, everything might turn out all right after all.

Jonas handed them each a bottle of water and a sandwich and then after they ate, poor Maureen ate several, they talked about finding a way out. When Will mentioned that he had been part of a rescue attempt at his friend Harry's house, Roger questioned him about where the house was and soon it became clear that Harry was the same person his assistant Angela was dating. Things were looking up. There was a possibility of their being rescued.

"Do you know if they had miniature drone planes that they could send in here and see us with?" The detective asked Will.

"Yes with cameras and microphones attached to them. Why have you seen one?"

"I think we did." Roger was feeling better already. A thought struck him and he asked Will, "If you are supposed to be rescuing us, what are you doing here, obviously as lost as we are?" Will sheepishly told them he had accidentally fallen through the frame after drinking a few beers.

"I didn't believe Harry when he was first trying to tell us about the frame. But there was this guy Mark, apparently he had convinced Harry that he had lost his girlfriend in here. Harry thinks his friend's kid may have fallen through the frame while playing at his mother's wedding. Before meeting up with us did you see a little kid and this Bethany woman?"

"Don't forget the young couple, Brian and Mandy, they were with the boy and Bethany." Maureen said as she stuffed another sandwich in her mouth. "I forgot, I really like peanut-butter and jelly sandwiches." She scraped peanut-butter from the roof of her mouth with her tongue.

Somehow having their group grow in number made each of them feel a renewed sense of hope. Since there was no better plan than Maureen's they each put one of their hands on the wall and moved parallel to it, in single file, at a speeded up pace. They did this for quite some time and then stopped to rest and formed a little circle and sat next to the wall. They were about to stand and resume their quest for an exit, when from above, they heard a whooshing sound and then something fell in front of them. It looked like a big pink object falling at a tremendous speed, past them and down. It caused them to feel a breeze as it went by and descended out of sight. Maureen freaked and squealed,

"What was that? Did you all see that? Oh my God, does this mean that we are on the edge of a precipice and could fall of an edge with the next step?" The four men were quiet for a time, the horror in her question causing the hairs to stand up on their skin.

"None of you have fallen down any precipices yet, so I would assume that we are not going to fall anywhere." Jonas's voice sounded calming and reasonable for only a second. Hadn't they all just witnessed that there were deeper places they could fall into? They all began to feel their sanity creeping away into the murky half-light of this place.

"We can't let this paralyze us, I think we should keep moving and hope for an exit or a rescue. The good thing is that someone is trying to get us out." The detective was shaken up, but felt it silly to just sit there and not move. They all stood and resumed their previous single file stance.

"Wait," it was Maureen again, "what if we are moving away from the rescuers, maybe we are making it harder for them to find us?"

"We shouldn't forget that there is more than one exit, so either way moving seems the best choice, what do you think Jonas?" Jake asked his older brother who nodded and said,

"Let's keep going."

Will was in the front of the line and he didn't say to anyone how hard it was for him to put one foot in front of the other. He hoped beyond anything he had ever hoped for before, that his foot would not encounter an empty space.

37.

Bethany, Mandy, Nicholas and Brian sat for a long time in front of the Mars Rover and waited for another talking session with their rescuers. They seemed to be waiting for a very long time.

****

Working in the confines of the corridor off the Smith brother's farm house felt a lot more cramped than working in Harry's house but there was a fever pitch of excitement in the air as each man set up his equipment. Since there was no need to use a harness Chuck was helping Doug haul in the heavy electrical chords down through the basement. They hooked up high intensity halogen lights along the ceiling of the passage. Having the bright lights on gave them a sense of cheeriness that the gloom at the end of the passage robbed from its occupants. Harry and Fred, who were in charge of the sound and camera equipment, worked on the drone plane hoping to be able to fly it toward the NASA robot. They were receiving strong signals from the robot and Mark, who had no particular job, was urging them to hurry and get the communications working as he was anxious to talk to Bethany again. Angela, who was standing close to Harry, saw that Mark was a distraction for the men, so took his arm and asked him to help her make coffee for the team. He agreed, making coffee or doing anything was far better than standing around feeling useless.

Standing in the kitchen together Mark and Angela felt a bit shy as they had only been introduced to each other a short time previously when Harry's friends had arrived to help.

"So," Angela said as she bent her curly head measuring out coffee grounds, "this all feels so unreal. Making coffee sort of seems out of place when you think about what is going on here. Tell me about Bethany." She gave an encouraging smile. She had broken the thin layer of ice between them, something she had learned to do while taking courses toward becoming a detective. Mark visibly relaxed and poured out his story, leaving out no details and finishing with,

"When I heard Bethany's voice back at Harry's house I'm embarrassed to say I actually fainted." He lowered his head and a lock of his light brown hair, falling into his thin face, was brushed aside. "I still can't believe she's actually alive after all this time."

"As I understand it, from what Jonas said, time runs differently there. So what seems forever to you may only feel like hours or a few days to the people in there. It's a difficult concept to hold onto, at least to me. But I can tell you it is really creepy in there."

"Tell me about it. I was too chicken to release myself from the harness to jump after Bethany and save her." Mark was flushed red with shame.

"Don't feel bad, you were all alone. As you can see Harry and his friends are brave because they are all together. They would possibly act as you did if they were by themselves."

"I would hazard a guess that they would have released themselves and gone after her. Fortunately they aren't facing the same dilemma that I did."

"Well there you go, every situation is different. See I'm worried about my boss and haven't a clue about how to contact him. I'm hoping he and Jonas hook up with your Bethany and they all come out together. It's very frustrating not knowing what's going on in there."

Angela's face wore a frown and she did indeed look very worried, but Mark wasn't the best at making conversation and didn't know what to say that might make her feel better. So he replied,

"The coffee looks about done why don't we take it down to the guys?" He carried the pot and Angela carried mis-matched mugs down the basement steps and into the brightly lit corridor.

Harry sat crossed legged, a microphone in one hand and his other hand occupied with turning dials on a transceiver. Static could be heard popping through the speakers he had tacked to the walls of the corridor.

"Brian can you hear me? Over." Harry said into the microphone as he held it in front of his mouth. He didn't get a reply so he fiddled some more with the dials and tried again. As he waited to see if he would be answered he looked up and saw that the guys had all stopped what they were doing and they were holding their breath listening along with him. Angela and Mark, carefully sidestepped over the snaking ropes and wires, and made their way to the group of working men. After Angela gave each of them a mug, Mark filled them with coffee, black strong and bitter. Enough to keep the sleepiest person awake for hours.

"Brian here. We hear you loud and clear. What do you want us to do? Can you hear me?" Harry got a reply, and gave a thumbs up sign to the small gathering of rescuers.

"Listen Brian, we have a plan. We'd like to try and have you walk out to us before we actually come in to where you are. By all accounts it's easier to get in, than it is to get out. But don't worry if this doesn't work we do have a plan B and will come in for you." Harry sounded a lot more confident than he felt. Chuck looked at Harry and mouthed, We have a plan B? Harry shrugged and continued talking to Brian.

"First we've rigged up a mini-drone plane to pick up the Rover's signal."

"How big is this plane?" Brian sounded excited.

"It's not that big, maybe two feet long, but it has powerful lights and microphones and cameras. If it's close to you there shouldn't be a problem seeing it, and it will see you."

"Oh," Brian sounded disappointed, "I thought you meant it could pick us up." There was a flurry of quick exchanges between Bethany, Brian and Mandy and then a loud childish question from Nicholas,

"Is my Mommy there?"

"Nicholas, buddy, remember me? Harry from your Mom's wedding? How's it going big guy?"

"Can I talk to my Mom? It's not so great where we are and I want to go home." Nicholas was trying to be brave but his little quavering voice belied his attempt. Then he burst into tears and both groups of people empathized with the little boy.

Harry swallowed a couple of times before replying in a voice that suggested absolute confidence, "You can be sure as soon as we get you out, both your Mom and Robin and your new dad Jimmy will be here and ready to take you home. Okay?"

Nicholas sniffed hard and answered, "Okay."

Mark, who understood the little boy's fear, was anxious to talk to Bethany again and asked the child if he minded letting him talk to her. For the next couple of minutes, while everyone in the corridor tried to look busy doing other things, like not listening, they waited while Mark talked to Bethany. Then Harry told them about the rescue plan.

Brian paced back and forth in front to the Mars Rover listening to Mark's voice as he talked to Bethany. When they were done Bethany gave them all a big smile as she wiped salty tears from her big black eyes. Mandy gave her a big hug, and the two heads, one so blond and one so raven, barely looked different in the gloomy light.

Harry's voice boomed through the microphones, "The drone is picking up the signal the Rover is broadcasting and so we will have it home in on your position. When it gets there, my good friend Fred, who is our expert on cameras and controlling the flightpath, will slow it down and circle around you. When you see it, all you have to do is follow it and it should come straight to us and we will be here waiting for you."

"How long do you think it will take it to get here?" Brian was just itching to leave the place.

"Well none of us is sure about that. We don't know how far away you are, but you should probably be able to hear its engine when it's getting close and we will be in touch through the Rover's mike the whole time."

Chuck who was still concerned about the Rover asked Harry to ask Brian if he thought he could carry the expensive, but damaged, machine out with him. Harry did and then they all heard Brian reply,

"Anything, anything you want. I'd carry the two gals and Nicholas along with the Rover if that what it takes to get out of here." They all felt a bit sorry for the young man. How would it feel to be that desperate?

Fred readied the little aircraft and the group in the corridor each silently hoped that the rescue would go without any hitches. None of them relished the idea of going into the place themselves.

37.

The morning after the Mark and Harry's friends had left his house, Alice was burning with curiosity about what had been going on in the house next to hers. To take her mind off them she decided to go on a shopping spree. She desperately needed a new bathrobe, hers was getting a bit ratty and worn. She was also going to get a couple of new sweat suits. She loved the new designs they came in these days. They were almost pretty enough to wear for occasions other than exercising, which was good as she didn't exactly exercise much more than walking to the end of her path to get the new spaper. She saw women wearing them in malls and even in restaurants. Why not? They were comfortable and she would buy several. She'd get matching sneakers as well. She loved shopping. Thanks to Harry she could spend more time shopping instead of sitting in an office cubicle working for a collection agency.

While she was at the mall Alice had her hair trimmed, as it had grown below the chin level length she thought flattered her the most. She bought three sweat suits, one powder blue to match her eyes, a grey one and a deep pink one that she thought suited her and complemented her coloring. She got three pairs of sneakers to match the suits and some gaudy costume jewelry to dress them up with. She was ready for any situation that might present itself to her. Maybe one of Harry's friends would like her looks and ask her out. She'd have to be sure Harry was not around when she sought an opportunity to find out about their marital status. She felt good.

Dressed in the pink sweats and pink sneakers, her hair freshly washed and wearing pink bracelets to match her outfit Alice walked down Harry's front walkway. Her ample chest bounced with each step. There were no cars in front of his house and Alice was sure no-one was in there but she wanted to check. Everything had been very quiet since she had watched his friends drive away. But maybe one of them had stayed behind and perhaps would tell her what had been going on. She rang the door-bell and waited. She rang it a second time putting her ear to the door to see if she could hear if anyone was coming to answer it. Nothing, so just because it was exactly the kind of thing she would be capable of, she turned the handle to see if the door was unlocked. Sure enough it was and Alice opened the door all the way and poked her head inside and called out to see if anyone was home. There was no answer. She thought, where was the harm if she just poked around a bit to get some answers to her curious questions? Just what had all the noise and bustle been about in this house? She walked in, then turned and closed the door behind her.

The house was built with exactly the same floorplan as hers. She checked the bedrooms first to see if anyone was sleeping. She found no one in them and so felt pretty confident that she was alone. Then she looked at the mess around her. Furniture was piled next to the walls and in the main room a big harness was dangling from the ceiling beam and hanging over what looked like a large picture frame lying nailed to the floor. There were pizza boxes and used paper plates and cups tossed in a pile in one corner of the room. The floors were scuff-marked where the men had walked with wet shoes and dragged lumber across them.

Alice walked around looking at the mess and even more curious than when she had first gone into Harry's house. What was that frame and harness for? She walked over to get a better look at it. She pushed the harness so that it swung back and forth over the frame. Whatever they had been up to was a mystery to Alice. She speculated that the harness was meant to be a swing for Harry's friend's kid, Robin. Who knew, the more she thought about Harry the weirder he seemed.

Well since I'm here I'll check out the swing. I can't remember when I last sat in one. I used to love to swing when I was a kid. She pulled the harness toward her and off to the side of the frame and wriggled into the seat. Pumping her legs back and forth she started to swing higher and higher, almost touching the ceiling. It was exhilarating, she laughed feeling like a child again. After doing this for five or six minutes she got a bit of a groggy feeling and stopped pumping her legs and began to slowly come to stop. She sat in the harness and it began to turn in a circle, stop, and twirl the other way. It was a pleasant feeling, reminiscent of her younger days. Eventually it stopped turning and was positioned directly over the frame. A lice unhooked the harness clip and jumped down onto what looked like a flat surface. But of course it wasn't a flat surface, it was an entryway to the other place and A lice plunged down through it like a heavily weighted anchor.

39.

Bethany was chattering away to Mandy about how the first thing she wanted when they were out of there was a long, long, hot shower. It was what Mandy wanted too. Nicholas didn't want a shower he just wanted his Mom. Brian wanted them to all be quiet so he could listen for the sound of a mini-plane coming toward them.

The speakers on the Mars Rover crackled into life and Harry's voice asked,

"Any signs of it yet? Our instruments indicate that it should be fairly close to you by now."

The small group of people craned their necks in every direction to see or hear the little plane.

"Not yet, we don't see or hear anything." Brian answered as he still kept turning his head hoping to see something.

"We'll keep monitoring the Rover's signal. I guess we just have to be patient, but it can't be too long now." Harry wanted to keep them all upbeat and hopeful. "We'll check back in a few."

Harry turned toward his rescue group and said, "I thought we'd have them following the plane back by now. It's been hours!"

"It seems like hours to us maybe, but maybe not hours to them. Remember I told you Jonas said time was different there." Angela was getting tired, and also thought they would have gotten the group out by then. She wanted to start looking for her boss but had a feeling it might be impossible to find him again. "Shouldn't we start figuring out a plan B?" She seemed deflated when she asked this. "Then shouldn't we figure out how to find Roger?" She looked at Harry with imploring eyes that had just a hint of tears in them.

Suddenly the speakers crackled into life and an incoherent amount of shouting could be heard over them. Over the babble Brian's voice could be heard over the squeals of the little boy and two women,

"It just flew over us and it's keeping on going. Did you see us?" Fred fiddled with his computer screens and the rear cameras picked out the little group of people, their heads all turned toward the departing plane. He turned it around and put it on automatic circle mode.

"It's coming back and flying around us." Brian put out his arm and pointed at it. Mandy pulled his arm down and nervously yelled at him,

"Be careful Brian, we don't need you breaking the plane as well!"

"Folks, folks calm down. We see you and what we want you to do is to follow the plane after we stop it from circling." Harry tried to inject a sense of calm into the hysterical squeals coming from the lost group. It was difficult to make them out clearly but from their demeanor it was obvious that they were in a state of exhaustion and scared, he knew he would be in that situation.

"Harry, ask them if they've seen Roger or Jonas." Angela pleaded.

Brian heard her and replied that they had only seen Maureen and had to leave without her because she was weak. The group in the tunnel looked at each other and Mark silently mouthed,

"Who's Maureen?" His question was answered with shaking heads. Then as if re-playing an episode from what seemed like a hundred years ago he said, "I bet she's the gal from the gallery. She lived in your house Harry, and she was the one who took the frame home with her after I first tried to get rid of it."

"Well I'm afraid we'll have to worry about her after we guide these guys home. We need to get moving." They all nodded in agreement and checked their equipment to be sure it was working properly. As an afterthought he said, "A person could make this rescue thing a full time job. Oh I forgot that's the Smith brother's job, and look where it got them! How would you be able to find all the people who are probably in there?" Mark feeling useless collected the coffee cups and took them back to the farm house. He needed to do something to make the time go faster while waiting for Bethany.

"Okay Brian I'm going to start the drone moving toward our direction and you need to let me know if you lose sight of it." Fred spoke into his microphone.

"And Brian you need to either carry or drag that Mars Rover along with you, or my ass is grass." This from Doug, his bushy beard quivered with each word. "Besides me needing it back it's still sending us a signal as to where you guys are."

To Brian, Mandy and Bethany it was disconcerting to keep looking at the plane and follow it. They had become used to looking down in the murky place so they could at least see a little where their footsteps led them. They also were walking faster than before, the plane was moving slowly but if it went too slow it might not be able to stay airborne. Since being found by the group Nicholas never worried where he put his feet, he was practically dragged along at whatever pace the rest happened to be going, or he got a piggyback ride from Brian. Now Brian was dragging the Rover thing along behind him so he couldn't carry Nicholas and Nicholas was getting tired of being pulled along and so he started to whine. No amount of reasoning or cajoling would shut him up so the group just put up with him and hoped the plane would lead them to the exit very soon.

40

Detective Roger Brown rubbed the back of his neck. It was getting stiff from his head jutting forward, attempting to see further through the gloom than was really possible. He felt some admiration for the woman Maureen, who he realized he had investigated as a missing person. At their next stop for a rest he asked her how long she had been down here. She didn't know but said it felt at least as long as a week, maybe more.

"It's probably a lot longer than that." Jonas said. Jake nodded agreement.

"Well what's the longest time you know for sure a person can last down here?" Being a detective Roger was the kind of person who needed answers. The unknown was something he needed to turn into the known. He received only shrugs from the brothers.

Will was starting to share the frustration he heard in Roger's voice. Maureen didn't have anyone close who would miss her. The brothers had each other and Roger had an assistant to worry about him, and he had Harry and his friends. He kept thinking the cell phone might be a way to contact someone and get a message to Harry. He wanted to try it again but decided to wait a while longer before doing so. The last time he tried the bars looked about to run out. Next time they stopped for a rest he would try one more time. He told the group of his decision and Roger said,

"There's no time like the present why not right now? Here hand it to me and I'll call Angela, my assistant."

Will wasn't about to give up the phone. He felt its weight in his pocket and put his hand around it, somehow it felt like a security blanket and if it ran out of power altogether then he felt that might mean that hope had run out as well. He shook his head no, at Roger. Maureen and the brothers didn't mind waiting until the next rest stop to use it. Each of them didn't want to face the possibility that the phone might be their last chance of finding a way out with the help of someone outside of this place. If there was no way to contact anyone, then they would feel abandoned. The brothers had no suggestions at all as to how to find an exit, so they all just plodded on hoping Will's friends or Roger's assistant would come through for them.

41

Harry had followed Mark up into the farm house kitchen. Mark voiced his frustration on how long it seemed to be taking to get Bethany and the others out.

"I feel like roaring down those basement steps on my Harley and riding with the lights blazing and picking her up and taking her back home." He said in an exhausted voice.

Harry's face lit up with a huge smile, one that practically made his eyes disappear into the laugh lines around them. He grabbed Mark and enveloped him in a breath-squeezing bear hug, pushed him away and gave him a slap on the back.

"In stealing a line from Henry Higgins 'I think he's got it.'" Harry shouted. Mark looked at him as a smile was starting to play around his lips as well, and he said,

"I do! What do you mean? Go in there on Hogs?"

"Exactly, and we could hook sidecars on them and get the whole group out in one fell swoop."

"It just so happens I have a couple of Harleys in my garage and they are in excellent condition. I often ride out to the countryside in Eastern Washington and take pictures for my landscapes. Sorry no sidecars though."

Harry who seemed energized anew seemed to infuse new energy into Mark as well. "Let's go out to my house and get them, we can stop at the Harley dealer on the way back here and pick us up a couple of sidecars." Mark suggested. At that moment Angela poked her head into the kitchen and saw the glowing faces of the two men and knew something was about to happen.

"Sidecars? What are you two talking about?" Angela asked as she sank wearily into one of the kitchen chairs next to the table. Harry walked over to her and put his arm around her shoulders and told her about the bikes.

"Mark and I will take his car back to his house and we'll pick them up and ride them here after we get a couple of sidecars for them."

"I'd like to come with you, is that okay?"

Harry rubbed her shoulders and said, "Well I think you would be more help here. We can keep in touch by phone and you can let me know how the guys are managing and tell me if they need us to bring in any other equipment. They're all professionals and you manning, or should I say 'girling' the phones for us, will be a great help." Angela nodded in agreement, a bit disappointed, her mouth drooped a little.

"Well I'll just fill the guys in on what we are planning and then we'll be off. It shouldn't take us more than about five hours, depending on the traffic and we'll be back before you know it. With any luck, by then you may have guided them out before we even get back, then we can try to find your boss." Harry said.

He went back to the men working in the cramped confines of the corridor and told them the new plan. They thought it was a great idea. Back in the kitchen Angela was alone, Mark had gone to warm up his car so Harry took this opportunity to give Angela a tender kiss without the eyes of his friends and Mark watching them. As he left Angela told him to drive carefully, the roads could be quite slick at that time of the year. "And hurry back." She added.

When Mark pulled onto to I. 5 going south to Seattle it was raining and starting to get dark.

"By the time we get to West Seattle, get the bikes and then back as far as the Harley dealers, they will be closed. Then we won't be able to get the sidecars." Mark observed.

"Y'know you're right." Harry answered. "Do you know if this dealer rents?"

"I don't. But you know what? We could save ourselves hours if we just stop there first and ask."

"Good thinking and if they don't, I'm not trying to sound like 'the man' but I could easily pay for a couple of Harleys and their sidecars if we needed to." Harry looked at Mark as he said this.

"For that matter so could I. In fact I am familiar with the manager of this dealership and so we could probably be back on the road in an hour. I'd leave my car there until this is all over with, then pick it up some other time." They kept driving and in a half hour Mark signaled a right turn off the freeway and drove into the parking lot of the Harley dealership.

They were instantly greeted by the floor manager and he remembered Mark quite well. It wasn't often you sold a guy two Harleys. The bikes were displayed in row upon row, leaning on their kickstands. They all gleamed with their polished chrome and shiny leather seats. The salesman was eager to make a sale, he hadn't had one all day and now here were two guys each wanting a bike and it was almost closing time. Who said there weren't any wishes granted? He had always wished to sell more than one bike in one day, now it was happening. And they wanted sidecars. There would be a nice bonus for him from this sale.

The bikes were filled with gas and had sidecars attached and were in the front of the sales room, waiting for the new owners to drive them away. Mark and Harry were being fitted with the correct sized helmets and goggles for the safest ride. Harry already had sturdy boots and luckily the dealership carried a line of boots for biking, so Mark bought a new pair of those. The manager agreed to keep Marks car in the service and repair garage until he could get back and pick it up. The salesman and manager had been curious as to why the two men wanted to buy Harleys at this late time in the day, but hadn't really been given a reason other than to say it was a spur of the moment decision. They weren't curious enough to jeopardize the sale by asking too many questions, after all a sale was a sale.

Harry and Mark sat on the giant motorcycles, clad in sturdy boots, helmets and goggles and huge grins on their faces as they roared the engines of the powerful machines. The whole transaction had taken a little over two hours and now they made their way to I.5 North. Angela would be happy that they would get back sooner than expected. The rain had stopped and they rode side by side, their huge lights making a wide swath of the road look as bright as day.

Half an hour later the two men pulled up to the farm house and the racket of the big engines could be heard throughout the house. It wasn't long before Angela raced out to meet them. She folded her arms against the chilly night and tilted her head to one side, her pretty curls reflecting highlights in the beams of the bikes.

"Those are new bikes aren't they?" She said excitedly. She had a big smile on her face and added, "Did you know that I have a motorcycle endorsement on my driver's license. I've never actually ridden a brand, spanking new one though. Mind if I take one for a quick spin?" She seemed in awe of the machines and to have completely forgotten why Harry and Mark had gone out to get them. Harry was amused by her excitement and reminded her that they were for rescuing, people, joy rides would have to come later.

"We'll have to take the sidecars off and reassemble them at the end of the corridor and just inside the other place." Harry said. Mark nodded as Harry went to get some tools.

"I guess you guys haven't actually gotten Bethany and the others out yet?" Mark asked Angela. She shook her head no. He added "I would have liked to have Bethany run out here rather than have to actually drive these things in there."

"As long as it's with Harry I would be happy to drive and you can keep in touch by radio." Angela seemed to like this idea. Mark thought for a moment before saying,

"No I definitely have to be the one to go in with Harry. It's my fault that Bethany fell in there in the first place. This is something I need to do."

"I do understand Mark, but if you change your mind I'd be happy to do it."

Harry re-appeared and he and Mark set about dismantling the sidecars. Angela went down to the corridor and moved as many of the ropes and cables to one side of the wall so the men would have an easier time pushing the bikes along. When she got to the end of the corridor she told the men that Harry and Mark were back with the bikes.

"Good, because I sure as hell thought we would have gotten them out here by now." Fred said pushing his glasses up onto his nose with his middle finger. "They sound very tired when we actually talk to them. The kid cries every time we open up the mikes to talk with them. And Chuck here seems to think all he has to do is run in there and he'll see them and carry them out himself." Chuck did a 'me Tarzan' thing while pretending to beat his chest with closed fists, but with very little enthusiasm. Angela detected a drop in morale. She looked at the bearded Doug who was crawling around checking the connections to the lights, he looked up at her and gave a thumbs up sign.

"I'm sure we'll be seeing them all coming out soon, especially now we can use the Harleys to get them." Angela said as Harry came into sight pushing his bike, followed by Mark. There were a few whistles and Doug said, "Sweet," as the bikes were looked over and admired.

Chuck and Doug needed to stretch their legs so they went back for the sidecars and helped to attach them to the bikes. Mark was anxious to let Bethany know that the cavalry was about to mount their rescue and a few minutes after contacting the lost group, he and Harry kick started the bikes, the noise was deafening in the small confines of the corridor, and roared off into the murky half-light. The red rear lights on the bikes quickly disappeared.

42.

Maybe it was because he was young and his eyesight was clear and sharp, or maybe it was because he was short and his eyes closer to the ground but it was Nicholas who saw the motor cycles' lights first.

"I can see the big white bunny rabbit. No I can see lights and I hear noise," his high voice piped, and in a few more seconds the others saw them too. They all jumped up and down and yelled. Brian let go of the robot and hugged Mandy and then turned and hugged Bethany and Nicholas. With a big sigh of relief he proclaimed,

"Thank God!"

The Harleys pulled up in front of the small group and Harry and Mark got off them. In the next second Mark and Bethany looked like they were welded together. Harry scooped Nicholas up and gave him a big kiss on the cheek and said,

"Remember me? I'm Harry." For a few seconds it looked as if little Nicholas had no idea who Harry was and his mouth turned down at the corners as his eyes threatened to leak tears, when suddenly his mouth changed course and smiled.

"You know my Mom." His little head turned from side to side and then tried to peek around Harry's back. "Is my Mom here? I know she's missing me!"

"Whoa, slow down little guy, we need to get you out of here first, and in next to no time we will have your Mom, Dad and sister giving you a welcome home party. Would you like that?" It seemed that he did as his head bobbed up and down in a 'yes' gesture.

"Okay you guys let's figure out how we are going to fit you all onto the bikes." Mark and Bethany seemed not to hear him so he gently pried them apart. Mark would not take his eyes of her and held her hand, and it was obvious that he never intended to let it go. Brian and Mandy were very anxious to get out and helped Harry put Nicholas and the Rover robot into the car on Harry's bike. Mandy went into Mark's sidecar and Bethany sat behind Mark with Brian behind Harry and they were ready to leave. But which way would they go? While the little group had been greeting each other they had lost sight and direction of the drone plane.

In a voice filled with frustration and not a small amount of fear Angela shouted into the mike.

"Harry, answer me. Can you hear us? We seem to have lost touch. Have you found them yet? Over."

There was no immediate reply. Fred typed instructions into his computer keyboard and checked his monitors. His equipment was all in working order and he told Angela and the men who were clustered around him as much.

"I think I'll have the drone fly in circles for a while, they may not be keeping up with it. I'm still getting signals from the Rover, but I'm not sure if it's moving or stationary."

Several hours passed by and Angela was hoarse from shouting into the mike and hoping for a reply. Periodically one of the group would leave and brew coffee and bring it to the rest. Their spirits would pick up for a bit but as time passed they began to worry about things like the bikes running out of gas, or Mark and Harry being as hopelessly lost as everyone else who had passed through the entryway to the other place. After three and half hours of nothing, finally their mike crackled and Harry's voice could be heard coming out of the loud speaker,

"We are on our way, all present and accounted for. We lost sight of the drone for a few minutes there be we see it flying in circles, time to head us in your direction now. Whenever you're ready Fred."

"Harry it's been hours since we heard from you!" Fred replied. "How is your gas?"

Harry must have been feeling very upbeat and in a joking mood as he replied, "I don't have gas! Oh you mean gas in the Harley. Well strangely, it reads full. We apparently haven't used any gas, but the bikes are purring along just fine."

"Okay well just follow the drone and I have a young lady here who is very worried about you and is jumping up and down and wants to talk to you." Fred handed the mike to Angela who gave him a big smile and told Harry to hurry on back.

Time seemed to drag for the people in the corridor but to Harry and his little group it seemed not to pass at all. They quickly turned toward the drone as it stopped circling and followed it on its straight path toward the corridor and the way out. Harry shouted to the people on Mark's bike to ask how they were doing, but he may as well have not bothered as his voice could not be heard over the sounds of the roaring engines.

Eventually the group waiting for Harry's return heard a muffled sound that quickly turned into a thunderous roar and then two powerful beams could be seen coming out of the murky half-light. The group began to wave, cheer and jump up and down. Not easy to do considering the narrowness of the hall and the cables strewn across the floor, but somehow they managed. The people on the bikes returned the waves and shouted back and Nicholas's little hand could be seen waving from behind the Mars Rover in the sidecar.

With their arms around each other Harry and Angela led the group through the corridor and then the basement up into the farm house kitchen. Mark and Bethany clung to each other as they entered the room and Brian held Mandy's hand and carried Nicholas. In the bright lights and warmth of the kitchen they all eyed each other as Chuck, Fred and Doug set about fixing them all something to eat. The supplies that Mark had brought in weren't stretching very far so Chuck left to go and buy more.

Seated at the table and looking very sleepy Nicholas asked, "Isn't my Mom here? I thought she would come and take me home."

"And she will just as soon as I call her and tell her you are safe." Harry thought how small the kid was and endearing and what a hell it must have been for him. He left the room and went out for some fresh air taking his phone with him.

43.

Harry gulped in the fresh cool air outside the farm house. It was almost light and he was surprised that a whole day had passed since they had ridden into the place for the rescue. A killdeer gave a haunting call as it flew somewhere off in the distance. He flipped open his phone and dialed his friend Jimmy's number. If Jimmy wasn't up yet he was sure his friend and his new wife Kathy would be more than happy to get up once Harry told them his news. His explanation of where Nicholas had been would be a lot more difficult for them to take.

"Harry I know you so well, so for God's sake tell me you're not joking." Jimmy's voice almost cracked as he said the words.

"Since you know me so well, surely you know I would never play a sick joke like that on you or anyone else for that matter. He really is here. I'll spend time telling you all about it later, but for now get a pencil and paper and write down the directions. It's actually easy to find the place."

Harry gave the directions and told Jimmy he thought it might be best not to tell Kathy about her son until they got to the farm house near Woodinville.

"I'll have to tell her and Robin something. It's not like we go for pleasure drives so early in the morning on a week day."

"I'm sure you'll think of something. He is asking for his Mom and I did tell him you would throw him a party when he gets home, so don't make me a liar, and I'll see you in a couple of hours."

Harry turned toward the house just as Chuck pulled up returning from the grocery store. Chuck's round red face had a big grin on it.

"You know I didn't really believe any of this was possible," he said as he handed a grocery bag to Harry. He reached in for a couple more and they went back into the house. "Once we get Will out, I swear this is the best adventure I was ever a part of. I'll be telling this story for years to come."

Once in the house Harry looked at the group of rescued people and felt a bit sorry for them. Mandy and Brian even though they were young, looked kind of grey and washed out, anemic even. Bethany, who was wrapped in Marks arms, looked as if she had been dragged through a hedge backwards her clothes were tattered and torn, her face dirty. And poor little Nicholas looked skinny, dirty and pale, a ghost of the shiny and clean child at his mother's wedding. Nothing a good meal and a long shower wouldn't fix.

They all sat at the table together and ate a huge breakfast that Harry's friends had fixed. Angela just played with her food as she wanted to go back in and find her boss, but there was no plan for that just yet. Harry asked Angela to take Nicholas to the bathroom and clean him up a bit before his mother saw him. He knew she was anxious about Detective Brown and he wasn't sure how to go about finding him. Cleaning up the kid might take her mind off the problem for a bit. But as always Nicholas was not about to do what anyone told him to do, only Mandy was good enough to help him get cleaned up. She did so willingly and couldn't wait for a shower herself, she didn't even care if it was a cold shower, any kind of shower would do.

"Dibs on the bathroom after you." Bethany said. She didn't mind waiting for it, she was with Mark again and still eating. "I never thought food could taste so good." She said to the doting Mark.

Driving north to Woodinville Kathy was badgering Jimmy about this strange turn of events.

"You could at least give me a hint of what we are doing out in this awful traffic."

She had been told to hastily dress herself and Robin and Jimmy had a big surprise for them. Kathy wasn't a morning person and having to dress in a hurry didn't put her in the best of moods. Robin, like her mother wasn't a morning person either and she was uncomfortably curled up in a ball trying to sleep. It was a shallow sleep as the seatbelt made it hard for her to get into a comfortable position. She gave up and joined with her mother asking where they were going.

Finally Jimmy said, "Keep your eyes peeled for the Woodinville exit, it should be coming up soon."

"What's in Woodinville?" Kathy and Robin chimed.

"We'll be looking for a farm a couple of miles away from there. That's all I'm going to say." He seemed to be enjoying himself.

"Oh no, you haven't gone and bought a farm in the middle of nowhere, have you?" Kathy sounded disgusted. "I hate the countryside. I don't want to live on a farm. What do you know about faming?"

"I said I wasn't going to say any more. But before you have a cow, get it? Cows live on farms. No I haven't bought a farm."

"I want to live on a farm. I could have a pony. None of my friends has a pony." Robin piped in.

"We are not getting a pony, where would we keep it? Jimmy just said he hasn't bought a farm, thank heavens. I'm sorry honey." Kathy told her daughter.

Jimmy stopped talking to the girls and started to check street signs looking for the one Harry had told him to turn on. He found it, like Harry had said it was easy to find, he drove a couple more miles and pulled up in front of the farm house. The sun was out, watery but casting a golden glow over the house. When they opened the car doors Robin and her mother covered their noses with their hands, the sun had warmed the rotting compost piles and they were generously wafting their arom a all around the house and yards.

"Thank god you didn't buy this place, why are we here honey?" Kathy looked mystified and Robin, muttered that she didn't really want a pony after all, farms were too smelly.

"I think that there is a surprise in this farm house, and it's all thanks to Harry." Jimmy said with a shy grin and the sun shining in his blue eyes gave them a sparkle that matched the tone of his voice.

"Harry bought a farm? He doesn't seem like a farming kind of person."

"I don't think he is."

'Well what then?"

The three of them stood at the door and Jimmy knocked loudly, they could hear loud voices and laughter coming from behind it. When the door opened they expected to see Harry, and at fist, because they were looking up, they didn't see Nicholas until he wrapped his little arms around Kathy's legs and said,

"Mommy."

45.

Kathy and Jimmy were in a state of shock when Harry pulled them into the house as Chuck, Fred and Doug got up from the kitchen table to make room for them. Brian, Mandy and Bethany told them about the strange place where they had been, Nicholas added important details such as his being very brave. The reality of having Nicholas back sank in and Kathy broke down and cried. She hugged the child as if she would never let him go.

The crowded kitchen became very hot as Doug stood in front of the kitchen stove and whipped up three extra plates of a hearty breakfast for Jimmy, Kathy and Robin. The aromas which had smelled so great when they were all hungry, now seemed too much a second time around. After they ate the table was cleared and Angela brought up the subject of how they would find her boss and the two Smith brothers. Harry was sick with worry about Will as well, and Brian and Mandy added that they felt bad about leaving Maureen behind. For the moment no one had any bright ideas. Jimmy wanted to stay and help in any way he could, but Harry didn't think there was much Jimmy could do, so it was agreed that he would take his family back to Seattle and keep in touch by phone. The whole group stood outside and waved the little family off as they left for home.

Brian and Mandy were becoming pretty hyped up about returning home and seeing their parents. Chuck who had been in charge of the climbing gear that wasn't needed at the farmhouse, offered to drive them to Seattle and drop them off at one of their parents houses. Harry agreed that it was generous of Chuck to do this for the young couple and asked if Chuck could check on his house since it would be on his way anyway. There was no reason for them to stay at the farm house any longer so they also left.

The house seemed satisfyingly quiet after the two departures and Angela cleaned up the kitchen and Bethany finally got to take a shower. Then they seriously felt inadequate as no one had a clue as to how to proceed with a plan for the next rescue.

Fred sat on the kitchen floor tinkering around with the Mars Rover's broken antenna. He wanted to get it back in working order if possible. If he could get it working right they could send it and the drone plane back in to see if they could spot Will, or the detective and maybe even the brothers. He also felt they owed it to Chuck to give it back to him in the same condition as he had brought it to them.

Harry went over to Fred and squatted down beside him and said,

"It would be fantastic if you could pick up some images of Will and the others. Do you need me for anything?" Chuck shook his head 'no' and continued to repair the damage. After that he needed to change the batteries in the drone and do some tweaking to make sure it was up to par.

"Then I think I'll go and check on the amount of gas in the Harleys. Want to go with me Doug?" Doug's brown eyes twinkled as his bushy beard bounced up and down with his nod.

Mark who was sitting at the table with Bethany on his knee suddenly jumped up sending her tumbling to the floor. He thrust his hand in his jean's pocket and pulled out his cell phone which was vibrating and faintly ringing.

"You guys might want to wait up a minute." He said to Doug and Harry who had instantly rushed to Mark's side. They both knew that there was only one setting on Mark's phone. It was keyed into Bethany's phone, but she was right there. So who was calling?

46.

Maureen was just about on her last legs. Will, Roger and the Smith brothers took turns in supporting her on their painfully slow walk through the depressing half-light. It wouldn't have been so bad if they knew for sure they were headed toward a specific exit point but each felt as if they may as well have actually been blind. Will hadn't shared with the others that he was really quite terrified of walking out into an empty space and falling into another place. The time between each rest seemed to be shorter and shorter as they were all tired. After the initial enjoyment of the sandwiches Jonas had brought, they were no longer hungry or thirsty, just tired and fed up with being where they were. They all agreed to sit and rest and maybe sleep for a while. The detective volunteered to stay awake while the others slept.

As the rest slept Roger helped himself to a bottle of water from Jonas's wagon and gazed down at the sleeping quartet. To keep himself awake he periodically circled the group and walked a short distance along the wall and then back to the sleepers. He hoped that he would detect a way out, but dared not go too far for fear the rest might awaken and go on in a different direction without him . He sighed and thought to get himself a sandwich when he noticed that Will had rolled over in his sleep and the cellphone had rolled out of his pant's pocket. He held his breath, bent down and gingerly reached for it. Like lightening Will was on his feet and his hand shot out like a striking snake and grabbed the phone from the startled detective. Roger nodded his head and said,

"You're right we should all be awake when you make the call."

"It looked a lot like you were intending to do it while we were all asleep." Will responded in a hushed and not too friendly voice.

"True I was thinking about it, but I would probably have waited until the rest of you were awake. I hope you noticed that I hadn't even opened it up." The detective's face was the epitome of open and honest intent.

"I'm sorry," Will said, "I just can't wait to get the hell out of here. I'm sure it doesn't matter who presses the redial button as long someone answers it. What's bothering me is that I'm afraid that no one will."

"I know what you mean." The detective sounded dejected.

The two men sat a very short distance from the group and talked quietly to each other about how long Will had known Harry.

"One thing's for sure, if anyone can get us out of here I'd bet my money on Harry."

"Well as I understand it, it's the two brothers here who are supposed to be the experts on that."

"Well excuse me for laughing but they don't seem that expert at their job or they wouldn't be as lost as we are. Calmer about it, yes, but they are as lost as we are." And Will was laughing, somewhat hysterically, it seemed to Roger.

"Let's wake them up and make that phone call. I've never been good at waiting!" Roger stood and paced around the edge of the sleepers.

When everyone was awake, Will said,

"Are we ready for what is possibly the last call we can make on this cell phone, the bars are just about used up?"

He pressed the re-dial button and waited.

"Who am I talking to?" Will asked as Mark said,

"Mark. Who is this?

"Is that the Mark who knows Harry?" Will's hand was shaking and his brow broke into a sweat. He hadn't realized that he was in such an emotional state. The rest of the group was clambering to get a turn on the phone until Roger boomed,

" Folks! QUIET. We don't know how long we will be able to talk."

Mark handed the phone to Harry.

When Harry established who the group consisted of he grabbed Fred and shared the earpiece with him. Fred was a man of few words and quickly set about picking up the cell phones' signal. Even when the battery ran down there would be enough residual power for them to lock a signal onto it. Harry noticed that the reception was breaking down so he yelled,

"Whatever you do keep the phone with you even after it goes dead. Did you get that Will?" Will didn't answer, the line was silent.

"Well people, this here is our lifeline even if we can't talk on it anymore." Will held the phone above his head moving his wrist back and forth for emphasis. He stood in the middle of a loose, small circle with each talking at the same time questioning him.

"How long will it take to get to us?" Maureen demanded to know.

"How will they be able to find us?" Jonas wanted to know.

"How do we know they will really come? Maybe we should keep moving and looking for our own exit." Jake didn't seem to have as much faith as Will and Roger.

"They'll find us, I have no doubt, and they won't give up until they do." Will's faith in Harry was born of experience. Harry had once rescued him out of a Baghdad sewer over in Iraq. If he came through for him there, he certainly would here. He told his companions as much.

47

There was an electric feeling of jubilation when Harry and Angela realized that their worries about the detective and Will and to some extent, Maureen and the Smith brothers were going to be salved. Just as Fred patted the Mars rover and declared it was as good as new, Chuck returned from taking Brian and Mandy home. Chuck's face turned into a huge grin and he patted Fred on the back and said,

"Thanks good buddy, I owe you one."

"Hold on Chucky, we have to put it back in service. We heard from Will. The brothers and the detective and the woman Maureen are all together with him, and we have a signal from a cellphone. I think we have a pretty good chance of following the signal on the bikes, and we can easily fit those guys on them. We probably only need to go in there one more time."

Fred and Doug put their efforts into checking out the drone plane as Harry tested the microphones, leaving Chuck and Angela without very much to do. Mark and Bethany were so involved with each other it never occurred to them to ask if their help was needed. Chuck and Angela went down through the basement, stumbled over the mess of wires and checked the gas in the Harleys. Both machines had only used about a quarter of a tank, so they topped them off and returned upstairs.

Without anything to keep them busy, Chuck and Angela went outside for some fresh air. It was already approaching dusk, the days were getting pretty short, and because of the cooling evening air the compost piles had stopped puffing out their foul smells. Chuck looked appreciatively at Angela, his hands in his pocket he rocked back and forth on his heels, took a deep breath and said,

"That Harry is one lucky guy finding a gal as cute as you. As soon as we get those other folks out, you'll be able to have him all to yourself again. I can't wait to get on that Harley, that'll be one sweet ride."

"Whoa there, big boy. I'm going in with Harry. You don't think I'm going through all that waiting for him to come back out of there, again, do you?"

"It's much too dangerous for you to go riding around in that miserable place. A little thing like you could get hurt."

"Don't think I can't take care of myself, because I can. I've been riding motorbikes for most of my life. I know how to handle myself."

As the discussion heated up Harry walked outside to tell them they were just about ready for the next rescue attempt

"Harry you need to talk to this little lady of yours and let her know that it's going to be you and me riding those Harleys to get Will and the others."

Harry folded his arms and tilted his head to look both at his friend and at Angela,

"Ideally we would all go in together, but Angela, honey, I think it best if Chuck goes with me. You understand don't you?"

Angela could feel the heat rising in her face, a sure signal that she was about to explode, but she didn't want to seem petulant in front of the two men so she swallowed a few times and said evenly, looking Harry in the eye,

"Harry, do you have you any idea how it felt to me when you went in there the last time? I was terrified I might never see you again. I have no wish to go through that a second time, so it will be me who rides in there with you."

Chuck raised his hands in a conciliatory motion and said,

"Never let it be said that I came between two lovers. Go ahead Angela, I'll be happy to stay behind with the guys. When you get back I'd love to ride on one of those suckers and see how fast I can make it go. Deal?" Angela replied by giving him a big hug and Harry a dazzling smile.

"You're a good friend, Chuck." Harry said as he patted the man on the back, "Did my house check out okay when you were in town?"

"Everything was the same as when we left, but the front door wasn't locked anyone could have walked right in."

"You locked it, right?"

"No I figured since everything was fine I'd leave it the way I found it.....Of course I locked it. You idiot." Chuck said as he pounded Harry's arm.

The three turned to go back into the farm house. Once inside the others were now here to be seen and neither was the Mars Rover or drone plane that had been worked on. They made their way through the basement to the corridor and the entry way to the other place where they were greeted with thumbs-up signs.

48.

Maureen was grubbing about in the bottom of Jonas's cart looking to see if there were any more sandwiches. She was out of luck they were all gone. She settled for a bottle of water.

"Do you think it will take them long to find us?" She wasn't asking anyone in particular, she just looked at Jake, Jonas, Will and Roger in turn as she tilted the bottle of water and took a sip.

"There's no sure way to tell how long it will take them," Will offered, "but you can bet they are working their butts off to get to us." He stood with his arms folded and his legs apart looking confident that they would be rescued. It was hard for all of them to stay in one place as they had unconsciously fallen into a routine. Sleep, waken then shuffle along looking for an un-seeable exit. It felt like that was what they had been doing all their lives. The gloom and quiet had robbed them of their ability to sense time and place. It was disconcerting but amazing how quickly each had adapted to their condition.

Will was absolutely right about the rescuers putting their all into the rescue operation. The drone was re-checked once Chuck, Fred and Harry were again in the entryway. Bethany and Mark remained in the farm house kitchen, making coffee and planning their happily-ever-after future. The Mars Robot was in excellent working order and of course the bikes were brand new. Fred was ready to track the drone and Rover on his computer screens and Angela, just to make sure that there was no doubt about the fact she would accompany Harry, was already seated on one of the Harleys and ready to go.

The drone plane was sending the Rover signals as it flew in ever widening circles looking to catch a glimpse of Roger and his group. Once they were spotted and hopefully communicating through the microphones, the plan was to send the Rover in and Harry and Angela would follow it. They were poised holding their breath and ready to kick start the bikes and roar off to the rescue. After half an hour had passed, and still no signs of the lost group were evident, they got off the bikes and went to stare at the computer screens. All that showed on them was a grey blur with the occasional indistinguishable object dropping down.

"I think we should move away from this wall and sit in a circle, so that when the drone reaches us it won't run into it." Will had obviously been running over this scenario while they had all been straining to hear if anything was coming for them. The prospect of wandering away from the wall wasn't very appealing to Maureen. It was the only thing that had given her hope, and calming enough to her, to protect her sanity. It took all four men to drag her away from it. They sat in a circle while Maureen, who now had nothing but empty space to touch with her outstretched hand, began wailing, sounding like a keening banshee. Will was appalled and put his hand over her mouth to shut up the noise, she bit him. When he pulled his hand away she continued on. They would never be able to hear anything over her wailing. Will was considering putting a gag over her mouth or even knocking her out, anything would be better than the awful sound coming from her. Jake, the younger Smith brother felt terrible for her and his inborn need to rescue the lost ones compelled him to move next to her and draw her to him so that her wails were smothered by his chest. They all visibly relaxed and craned their necks listening for the sound of the drone that Will had assured them they would hear once it got close to them.

"You'd think we would have seen something by now, it's been a couple of hours. I wonder how big that place is anyway." Chuck said. The group hadn't noticed Bethany and Mark making their way down the corridor, with coffee and cookies, so were surprised when Bethany's voice answered,

"Well it must be pretty darned big because I fell through in New York and here we are in, or should I say, near Seattle." They all looked at her. The small proclamation expanded their ideas of the confines of the place to world-like dimensions.

"Mmm, the search could take forever." Fred groaned. "I'm not sure how long I can keep my equipment tied up in this project." He took his glasses off and rubbed his hands across his eyes before replacing them.

"We can't give up!" Angela's voice was unnaturally high.

"No, no, no we won't give up. Maybe this is a good time to figure out how long we should commit to this search. We can all give it one more day but perhaps we should decide that we stop looking after, say, a week?" Harry said as a look of despair clouded Angela's face.

Fortunately they didn't have to think too much about abandoning the search because Chuck said, "Does that look like a circle of people sitting down?" He pushed his face closer to the screen as Fred worked the remote control for the drone.

"Hang on I'll have it make a couple of tighter circles." By the time Fred had the drone circle above the group they had all stood and were wildly waving their arms.

Angela breathed a sigh of relief when she saw the detective, as did Harry when he picked out Will's blurred features. They sent the little Mars Rover in and Harry and Angela got back on the bikes and rode in after it, following a short distance behind. Its fastest speed was only a couple of miles an hour so their progress seemed agonizingly slow.

49.

Maureen had stopped her wailing when Jake had jumped up to wave at the drone as it circled above them. Things that hadn't bothered her before began to gnaw at her. Would she get her job back? Where would she live? Someone else probably had her house. And then she thought that those things didn't matter any more. When she got out of here she would possibly find out if she still had any money in her name and go on a long tropical holiday. She would go to a place with blue skies and a warm sun. Just the thought of it perked her up and she jumped up and down and waved at the drone along with the rest of them.

As Harry and Angela puttered along behind the Rover on their powerful bikes they noticed the streams of air carrying the garbage along. Harry hadn't noticed it the first time he had ridden in there as his eyes were mostly concentrated

234

on watching the drone. But now he was curious about where they were going. He wished he dared follow one but that might mean that they wouldn't be able to find Will and the others. They followed the Rover for what felt like hours. There wasn't a whole lot to talk about because they couldn't hear each other over the sounds of the engines. The best they could manage was to look at each other and smile occasionally. Following the Rover and keeping his eyes glued to it through the gloom gave Harry a bad headache. He snapped to attention though when just ahead of them one of the garbage laden streams stopped flowing forward and formed into a whirlpool that seemed to plunge downward. Had he not noticed it they might have fallen into it. They drove around it and almost lost sight of the Rover. A new worry entered their heads, what if the Rover fell into a hole? How would they ever find the others? They hadn't spoken these worries aloud but they both knew what the other was thinking when they looked at each other. Harry was experiencing the same dread of moving forward, be it ever so slowly, as Will had when he was walking along following the wall.

Will was straining to hear some sound that might indicate that the rescuers were getting close to them. The drone continued to circle around them and they were getting used to its' mosquito like buzzing, so much so that they no longer seemed to hear it, so another sound would surely indicate that help was very close. The little group of people had become so tense with the strain of listening when they did finally hear the roar of the Harleys they weren't sure from which direction the sound was coming from. They all faced in one direction only to be surprised when the bikes pulled up behind their backs.

Angela was the first off her bike and ran to embrace her boss.

"Roger, truly, I thought you were gone forever."

"You can't get rid of me that easily," he said returning her hug.

Will and Harry were pumping each other's hand in greeting and looking very happy to see each other.

"You can bet if you ever warn me not to lean too far into something again I'll take your warning to heart and not do it. You always seem to be getting my butt out of messes." Will's voice was very sincere. He pushed Maureen forward, she had been standing behind Will, and he introduced her to Harry.

The detective put his arms around the Smith brothers pushing them toward Harry and telling him who they were. Their friendly round faces were like beacons of light as they grinned and profusely thanked Angela and Harry for being so brave to enter that unfriendly place and rescue them. Harry shook their hands and said,

"No problem, but I wouldn't want to make it a habit, coming into this place is really freaky. What say we all get the hell out of here and back to the land of the real and expected." They agreed the sooner they went back the better. But Harry had a few questions that he wanted answered and first asked the brothers about the streams of air carrying garbage.

"We're not sure about them but we thought it was a good way to keep the place clean. We fill quite a few black garbage bags with litter every week." Jonas replied.

"We did notice that they shift, stop moving and then another starts up and goes in a different direction. But we didn't know they did that before we came in here." Jake added.

"What about the whirlpools, they appear to go downwards?"

The brothers looked at each other and shrugged. Jonas said,

"We didn't know they could do that."

"Well they can, so everyone keep your eyes peeled for them. We don't want to fall in them." The jubilation faded and was replaced by looks of dread and fear.

After the stunned silence they began to arrange themselves on the bikes. Harry had Will and the younger Smith brother cram themselves behind him with Maureen in the sidecar. Angela Had Roger sit behind her and Jonas in her sidecar.

The drone was still circling above them and the Rover had stopped once it reached the stranded group. Harry assumed that Fred and his group were seeing them on their monitors and would start the machines on their return trip once he saw they were all seated on the Harleys. He waved at the camera on the Rover and expected it to begin to move immediately, but it didn't.

50.

Chuck was smacking the back of one of the computer monitors as if that would clear the static white snow that was all that could be seen on both monitors. His face was flushed with frustration, he didn't understand how these things worked as he was more of an outdoor type and didn't know much about electronics.

"Don't do that Chuck, you'll break it and then where will we be?" Fred admonished his companion as he rapidly typed new commands into his computer.

Doug was crawling along the snaking lines of wires and checking to see that none of the connections were loose. Everything looked okay to him so he went back to the farm house and out to the big power truck to see if everything was still in working order there. That checked out just fine as well. He went back down to join the others.

Mark and Bethany were standing and watching the monitors, willing them to burst back into life, like a father teaching his kid to drive and feverishly pumping his imaginary brake. Their efforts seemed to be as ineffective as the laboring Fred. That is until Fred dramatically raised his index finger and with the others watching he said, "Voila," as he hit the Enter key and the screen filled with the figures sitting on the bikes waiting for the Rover to go into action. Sure they were a bit

238

blurred but there was no doubt about who they were, and they waved with relief as the little Mars Rover began its journey toward the exit.

Angela and Harry started the engines and they were off. Everyone kept a sharp lookout for the whirlpools Harry had told them about, but no one spotted any. They could all see the strange streams of garbage. The journey became long and boring, the slow progress they made while following the Rover was monotonous and Harry and Angela had a hard time staying awake. They noticed that their passengers were, one by one, falling asleep. They had to keep going because they couldn't let the Rover disappear from view. Harry was slightly ahead of Angela so didn't see the whirlpool appear just behind him but he heard her shriek his name. He looked behind him and couldn't see her with Will and Jake blocking his view. Will slipped of the Harley and yelled to Harry telling him to cut his engine. Harry did and he and Jake jumped down to see what was wrong. Angela sat on her bike a look of terror on her face. Her sidecar, with Jonas in it, was hanging over the edge of a spinning whirlpool. The detective had his arms around his assistance's waist and was leaning in the opposite direction of the gaping hole trying to shift their weight so they didn't all fall in.

Because the motorcycles moved so slowly Fred had guided the drone back to the entry way and set it in a box ready for taking it home.

"I can't believe how long it's taking those guys to get back here." Chuck said as he watched the empty computer screens. "Fred can't you have the Rover move backwards so the camera is on them so we can see if they are following it."

"What a fool I am for not thinking of that." Fred yelped. He typed in some extra information the Rover whirled around and the camera barely picked out what looked like stationary shapes.

"They're not moving. Make it go back towards them so we can see what's going on." Chuck's voice was panicky.

"Calm down I'll send the drone back in and have it circle around them. Maybe we'll get a better picture from its cameras."

When the pictures came in they were frantic to get some help to them, but it was too dangerous to go running in there blindly. Chuck was willing to do just that, but both Fred and Doug persuaded him not to be so rash.

"As a last resort you and I could tie ropes around ourselves and go as far as they reach, but only if they can't figure this one out for themselves." Doug said to Chuck. Doug knew just how his companion felt, how they all felt, when they saw the predicament Angela was in.

Desperation for the woman Harry had fallen in love with gave him the strength of ten. That, and the combined efforts of Jake and Will, the three men were able to drag the bike and sidecar away from the edge of the hole and get it back on firm ground. Angela was so shaken up she said,

"Maybe Chuck should have ridden this bike instead of me."

"Nonsense, you did a great job, it could just as easily have happened to me instead of you." She smiled weakly at him, and then Will said,

"Hey Angela, why don't you take my place and sit behind Harry, and I'll drive your bike the rest of the way back."

Harry was vigorously nodding his head and Angela didn't even argue, she was just relieved that she hadn't lost Jonas.

Cheers went up at the entryway as the group saw the Harley dragged out of harm's way, although from their vantage point they couldn't really tell what the danger had been, and the little group started on its way again. They could now see them moving as the Rover moved in reverse and kept the cameras on them. It didn't feel more than fifteen minutes to Harry's group, but to the people in the corridor it was three more hours before they heard the first chugging sounds coming from the Harleys. When they finally came into sight the yelling from both groups was ear splitting. There wasn't much room for all of them jumping up and hugging each other. The one in the worst shape was Maureen, and even she managed to act excited.

Angela hadn't realized how much strain she was under, worrying about her boss, the detective and the older Smith brother Jonas, until they were all back in the Smith brother's kitchen and then her knees gave out and she was shaking and just had to sit down and collect her thoughts. While they were waiting for the group to return Mark and Bethany had gone out and bought a case of champagne. It was served in the brother's mis-matched coffee mugs. After they had all given each other little toasts they sat down to decide what would be done about the strange place the brothers protected the entrance to.

It was agreed that the brothers should continue to do what they did and none of them would leak the secret of their job to the general public.

"I for one will never speak about the place to another soul, I just want to forget it even exists." Maureen announced. "And I certainly won't be poking my head through any old picture frames that's for sure."

"I'll have a difficult time explaining what I and Angela have been up to lately, but I'll think of something plausible." Roger said seriously. "We need to get hold of the young married couple and let them know not to broadcast anything about the place they had been in." He added.

They all agreed that it wasn't a good idea to let anyone know about the place. They each made their plans to return to their old lives. Harry felt bad about Maureen not having a home to go to and offered to help her find another place.

51.

Harry and his friends, with Angela's help, set about cleaning up the mess in his house. Chuck and Will took down the harness and gathered up cables and ropes and put them in their cars and trucks. Fred returned the Mars Rover in good running condition back to Chuck who drove the power truck and Rover back to where they belonged, and then finally everyone was gone except Harry and Angela who said they would finish cleaning up and the rest of the house.

When it came to removing the frame from where it had been nailed onto the ground Harry told Angela to stay way back as he didn't want to lose her. She laughed and knelt beside him with a screwdriver and helped him pry the nails out that were holding the frame in position. As she went to pry a second nail the tool accidently flew out of her hand and landed in the middle of the frame. Except it didn't disappear it just landed on the white surface and rolled to one side. They looked at each other and both put their hands onto the white space expecting them to disappear, but they didn't. They quickly pried the frame up from the floor and looked behind it. It was just a frame with white gesso, a blank surface ready to be painted.

"Unbelievable. The entry way has gone." Harry looked at Angela, and she at him.

"I think we should tell the others. I'm going to call the Smith brothers and see if they still have their exit." Angela said. Harry agreed and waited while the brothers went to check. After five or so minutes they were back on the phone. They still had their entry way at the end of the corridor and there was an extra amount of garbage that they needed to get cleaned up.

Harry and his friends, Angela and her boss, and Nicholas and his family had a party in Harry's back yard. They had a bonfire and burned the frame and after that their lives carried on as usual. Harry and Angela married and she still worked for Roger and Harry continued writing his book. For the next couple of years they met to celebrate the anniversary of their getting out of the strange place. For each of them the experience seemed less and less real and as time went by they rarely even thought about it.

52

A lice landed so hard it knocked the wind out of her. She looked down at herself and her new pink sweatsuit was hanging off her in ribbons. It looked like it had been through a paper shredder. She thought she had seen people as she was plunging down but that might have been an illusion as she had been moving very fast. She got unsteadily to her feet and noticed that she was surrounded by a bluish mist. It could be smoke for all she knew but she didn't smell anything burning. She put her hand out in front of her and the blue mist swirled around it. She couldn't see anything beyond her hand, and her feet not at all. She called to see if there was anyone there but got no reply.

"This is that asshole Harry's fault. He deliberately set a trap for me. He's probably around here somewhere waiting to frighten me. She took a hesitant step and thought she saw a shape in the blue gloom. She moved toward it thinking it was Harry, and she was so mad she thought she'd belt him one when she got to him. But it wasn't Harry, it was a white rabbit about the size of a bulldog with red eyes and fangs. It hopped toward her and snatched at a piece of her shredded sweat pants. She turned, a shrill shriek escaping her lips, and ran blindly into the blue mist.

End.

www.ingramcontent.com/pod-product-compliance
Lightning Source LLC
Chambersburg PA
CBHW050734180626
46814CB00002B/754